The Great Portal Wars Trilogy
Book 2

Doorway to Destiny

Pauline Marquez

All content by author Pauline Marquez
Edited by Laurie Larsen
Cover Art by Balakumar Karunanidhi
Formatting by Polgarus Studios
Published in the United States of America

ISBN: 978-0-9909787-7-0 (Print)
ISBN: 978-0-9909787-8-7 (ePub)
ISBN: 978-0-9909787-9-4 (Kindle)

ACKNOWLEDGMENTS

Writing the second book to this "Great Portal Wars Trilogy," has been such an experience for me in the life of all my writing and imagining. I did not want it to end. Luckily, I have the making of book 3 to look forward to. This book took me away as I wrote the incredible adventures of unending suspense that I desire to share with all who will read it.

The Lord gave me the strength and the wisdom to write this book. I could not have written this any other way. So first and foremost, I thank Him for every word in this book.

As always, I must thank my parents, Tony and Nancy Miosi. My father is a pillar who always stands strong in my life. My mother helped with pre-editing before it went to the actual editor. Her insight and willingness to step in when I needed the help will forever be appreciated. In this book, my daughter, Rebekah, stepped in and gave clever ideas in ways I did not see. Her advice tremendously helped to make this book what it is today!

To my sister, Lisa, well what can I say? She helped me in bountiful ways and when I thought I'd have to set this project aside, God used her to get me through! Thank you for your faithfulness sister and your genius creativity and promotional skills.

Thanks to my new editor, Laurie Larsen, for her meticulous gift of making sure that the reader gets what they deserve, a sound and wonderful flowing story. Thank you for your incredible knowledge and hard work Laurie! I could not have done this without you!

Thank you, Balakumar Karunanidhi, for your help with the book cover. Even though you were in the middle of so many transitions in your life, you made time for this and I appreciate what you did. I simply love the cover!

I must continue to thank Emilie McDowell for her continued help with the ongoing website. It will always be appreciated!

My continued thanks to all of my extended family and friends as they all encouraged me to not give up when times were tough as I worked around the clock. All of you gave me the strength and endurance I needed to get through to the end.

Thank you and God bless you all!

Contents

Chapter 1
Adriana

Expecting her daughter to be asleep by now, Adriana anxiously got dressed in the darkness of her bedroom. It had become her custom to dress with no light so Jen would never suspect anything. She grabbed hold of the doorknob and opened it as quietly as possible. The creaking sound from the hinges caused her to grimace in disgust. *Darn door!* What made matters worse was the sight of Jen's door left wide open, which normally was closed at night. Adriana tiptoed over to the doorway of her daughter's bedroom and then stared down at her sleeping daughter. Feeling assured that the creak hadn't woken her; Adriana smiled, filled with excitement at the thought of meeting her new friend in the middle of the night.

He had pressured her into bringing Jen in order to meet her; in fact, he had practically demanded for it to happen. Looking at her sleeping daughter, the desire to open her mouth and whisper Jen's name was far more tempting than ever before. Perhaps it was time that Jen knew the truth about what really happened to John. She reached out her hand toward her daughter but then suddenly drew it back. Feeling selfish, she wanted just one more encounter with the stranger before bringing Jen in, just to be sure that he would be there this night. Adriana determined that if she had to come back and get Jen, she would. By the end of this night, Jen would indeed come to know the truth. But for now, Adriana moved away from Jen's doorway, walked through the living room and kitchen, and made her way quietly out the back door. Adriana hurried past Old Sam's rickety house and upon seeing the path, she dashed in.

The dirt on this trodden path gave way with less resistance now, as if to welcome Adriana to a dreaded trap. Like frozen lightning bugs scattered among the brush, the faint glow of beady little eyes stared silently in cautious fear at the intruder walking through their forest. They knew who it was that walked in the dark of night, looking for things that ought never to be found; even the untamed in the forest knew better. She walked expectantly, waiting. Then it hit her, the force of his summoning took hold of her, enwrapping her mind in senseless catatonic behavior. As each step passed the desire to feel him grew with an intense passion to the point where only one thing mattered; seeing him again. Like a sudden invasion, the erotic presence of this mystical being began to build, enveloping much of the forest. With quickened senses, the animals near the wandering woman fled away, hoping to find some hidden place of protection from the mysterious presence that would undeniably haunt them all. Every living thing with a beating heart had run away; all but one, all but Adriana. Her heart throbbed with intense palpitations as she surrendered herself to the senseless uncanny desires of the unknown.

Like a tender wave of a friendly fire, his presence drew her nearer. Her spirit quivered as if trying to warn her of imminent danger, but she quickly beat it into submission. With baited breath, she walked on with a quick stride, anticipating and longing. What she was doing was rash and impulsive, but Adriana justified to herself, *he is my only hope.*

Closing her eyes, she surrendered completely to the will of his presence, letting him guide her wherever he chose to lead. Through twisted paths she blindly walked until she ended up in a pit of intertwining trees deep in the secret place of the forest, and that's where she always had to wait for him.

Chapter 2
Him

As soon as she came to, her eyes gazed at the familiar pit of trees surrounding her. The tree trunks braided around one another several feet above her head, creating an impenetrable cage. She was trapped. Adriana never understood how she came and left that magical place, for she always had to surrender her mind to him in order to come and go. She felt vulnerable, but she had slowly grown to trust this stranger more and more. The branches swayed fiercely and then suddenly at the center of the pit, a glowing portal appeared, deep blue in color.

From within the glow, a man emerged. Knowing exactly where she'd be, he glared into her eyes with a strength that penetrated to her soul. Her eyes fixed on him, unable to move. His golden-like skin accented the flare of color that came from his eyes. She'd never seen skin that color on any other. His face was perfect, his golden-brown hair delicately draped down past his shoulders. He always seemed to wear the same casual clothes; jeans with black casual shoes and a white collared shirt. For just a moment, he gently smiled at the woman as he came out, but then his expression shifted to grave concern, ultimate betrayal as he looked around their secret sanctuary for the girl. The disappointment that emanated from him penetrated Adriana, causing her lips to quiver as an unnatural guilt took over and she tried to justify herself.

"I—I just wanted to be sure you would be here, before I bring my daughter to meet you for the first time. I mean, I didn't want her to think I was crazy or something in case maybe you couldn't come tonight."

The man stared at her as she blabbered away, and he marveled once more for a moment at the makeup of humans; how pathetically frail and worthless they all were to him. His endless vexation for humanity kept his fury smoldering and his end game in focus. He loathed this woman and everything about her. Yet, here he was, being surreptitiously knavish in an attempt to entrap her, so he could use her for his own evil purposes. And the need to get a hold of her daughter was the only thing that really mattered to him. He held back his fierce desire to claw away at her soul and forced out a fraudulent smile instead, giving the perfect impression that he understood her.

"I understand, Adriana. I know how difficult this has been for you. But we are close to finding him, and we have you to thank for that. I commend you for your bravery. But the time has come that we need Jen as well. We can go no further without her help."

Pride invaded Adriana's heart and she knew what she needed to do. "I will go get her. By the end of tonight, Jen will be helping us with this."

The man smiled. *Perfect,* he thought to himself.

Just then the portal reappeared and the man's smile disappeared. "Adriana, I need to go. A disturbance where I come from has been reported. But I promise you, I will be back tonight. Go quickly and get your daughter. Bring her to me and hurry. I need to find out what my enemies are up to now."

Before waiting for her to respond, he sent her into a catatonic state. The next time Adriana came to, she was at the edge of the forest, her house not too far away. She ran to the house, eager to wake her daughter and bring her into the forest.

Chapter 3
Jen, where are you!?!

It was like a dream; it couldn't be real. Adriana's body stiffened as if she were a corpse staring blankly into her daughter's room. Empty bed, missing shoes; it could only mean one thing. *No, she couldn't have! She was asleep. I made sure of it before I left.* Her head shook side to side in denial of the obvious truth. "No, no, no! Jen! Jen, baby, where are you?" She stumbled away from the doorframe of her daughter's empty room. She thought of the light, how it took her John….did it come back and take her daughter too?

The screen door exploded open and crashed against the siding as Adriana catapulted out of the house, barely touching a single step. Enraged, she raced toward the woods, toward the only one that could help her now.

As she reached the forest's edge, Adriana paused and looked back at her house in the distance. The lights on, door left open; everyone would wonder what had happened to them. She shivered at the thought of the gossip the neighbors would come up with. But she no longer cared what they had to say. They were not there for her, not when she needed friends. Adriana made a decision that night that she would never go back until her family was restored. The regret of not bringing Jen sooner was gnawing away at her now. How she wished she would have listened to him. With emboldened ambition, she turned to the forest and followed the twisted path. After a short while, she became catatonic and did not come to again until she was back in the lair made of twisted trees. He was already there, waiting for her.

As soon as their eyes met, shame overwhelmed her, and she began to sob miserably. The man simply looked at her as he walked over to her. He placed his hand on her shoulder as if trying to console her.

"I'm not mad at you for your blunder and poor misjudgment. I couldn't expect you to understand all that's going on, and that is why I have come to you; to help you. I do know why it is you're crying. When you went home tonight, you found an empty bed, I presume?"

He waited, forcing her to respond so she could sink further into her sorrow.

"Mhmmm," she finally mustered amongst her tears and parched throat.

"The report I received not too long ago was indeed very disturbing and unfortunate news. Not too long ago, my realm was greatly shaken by the entrance of another earthly human. I think we both know who that was." He dropped his hand from her shoulder and placed both his hands in his pockets, giving her time to feel the shame for not bringing Jen to him earlier. He wanted her to become desperate, and it was working perfectly. Guilt raged inside of her and she looked up like a helpless slave begging for forgiveness but willing to take any punishment.

Adriana tried to speak, "I, I'm so sorry," she sobbed, "I should've earlier tonight, but we argued because she got into trouble at school and I left without her at first. I didn't know she followed me. Perhaps…perhaps she's still here in the forest."

The man glared at her and shook his head. "We already have confirmation, that beast in the portal must have deceived her. It now has her, and I'm sure it will do whatever it can to brainwash her, and make me to be the villain, as it did your husband, John. He's caused so much trouble in our world." He paused and looked sadly toward the ground. "I'm not the villain here, Adriana. And now this thing has your daughter."

The man circled around her until he was standing directly in front of her; placing both hands on her shoulders, he looked directly into her eyes. "Look Adriana, the work you've been doing here in this sanctuary has been a great help. Over time you have slowed him down and we are to the point where he can soon be found, but it's time for a greater measure to now be taken. Have you thought about the offer I extended to you earlier?"

Adriana nodded and answered him feebly, "Yes."

"And?"

"Yes, I will go with you. But I need to know just one thing before I go."

"Of course. Anything, my dear."

"What do I call you? In all our conversations, you've never told me your name."

The man half-smiled. "That is because I go by many names, and I wish not to confuse you. But to satisfy that curiosity of yours, you may call me Liel. That should suffice."

With that, he backed a step away from her and reached out his hand for her to grab. The blue glow left the walls and focused once again in the center of the pit, close to where they were standing. "Then take my hand, Adriana, and together we will destroy the portal beast that took your loved ones and recover them by any means!"

Adriana grabbed his hand, and the two vanished. From that day forward, she committed to helping Liel. He used his 'special methods' and taught her how to explore the worlds of Earth through the consciousness of only her mind. Adriana was a fast learner; there were many times she felt she had found her husband John's consciousness, but he could not tell it was her and John defended against the attacks time and time again, leaving Adriana exhausted.

Liel pushed her far beyond her limits, leaving her passed out and lifeless by the end of each session. To show compassion on her, even though he despised compassion altogether, Liel sent aids to her side that pampered her as if she were royalty, adorning her with fine gowns and jewels beyond her wildest dreams. She was given a beautiful room within his castle deep under the ground in one of the hidden worlds of Earth.

The original name for this world was Free Earth, but Liel had conquered it long ago and renamed it with his own name. So now it is known as Liel's Earth. The furniture in Adriana's room was fashioned from gold and silver and a bed one could sink into as if sleeping on clouds. After recuperating from a session, Adriana would return with greater determination and a relentless passion to fight harder every time. She learned fast, and found ways to seek out John faster each time, waging constant war on his mind. Little by little, she tore down his defenses, and thus brought the day that the Skeign army was able to find John in Shadow Earth. Unbeknownst to Adriana, they took him and carried him down into the depths of their deepest and darkest of dungeons.

Chapter 4
John

The putrescent smell of the slow decomposition of rotting flesh smoldered in the air of the Skeign's dungeon. Shrieks and whimpers of the condemned were endlessly heard by those who were trapped. Pleas for death went unheard as their suffering and torment continued on and on. The Skeign were pleased with their handy work; it fueled their repulsive appetite for more wanton pleasure. So that's why it was with great intimidation that the Skeign creature assigned to interrogating John stomped down the hall toward his cell for more than a dozen times now. A dozen attempts to abstract from the mere human's mind what it needed, and now a dozen times, failure. What was it with this man's strength to resist, the monster did not know. Never before had a human lasted even one round, let alone twelve. It growled in disgust at its humiliating failure. Another flop this time would seal its fate with the Master. The interrogator approached John's cell with a new round of hideous, mortifying thoughts of how to breach the man's mind without killing him. It growled in contempt and slammed the cell door with a loud, resounding thud that vibrated down the hall, the fate of one or the other lying in the balance.

John's body tensed and shuddered at the sound of the slamming door, igniting a world of oncoming pain and agony. Up till now, he had been able to keep the Skeign from seizing his mind and stealing all his secrets. But he was weak, thirsty, and fading fast. Even he knew it was only a matter of time now. Though he couldn't think of places he could transport himself to, he at least had the ability to lock up his memories and start a defensive wall of fake memories in case there was a successful breach. With shortened breath and gripping fear, John waited.

Jen, hurry! Find me, please! A screeching howl emitted from John as the Skeign's probing tentacle entombed his head, electrifying every nerve in his body. The Skeign was relentless in its attacks, using John's nerves against him, the monsters' biggest source of torture. John's eyes bulged in horror as the feeling of a million knives stabbed every area of his body. Blood stained his restraints as his body twisted and contorted uncontrollably.

JEN! HELP!

Chapter 5
And so the Story Begins

From a distant hill, Iyon peered down into Tolare; the sound of music, laughter and dancing rang through the streets. During such a time of war it should have been a pleasing sound to hear for a change. Iyon tried to take in the joy, but it was something he had always struggled with ever since the day the Warrior Horses fell. Until recently, he had thought that he was the last one. The visions of Malum haunted his memories and the mystery of not knowing who he was pained him. Music faded as Iyon began the agonizing process of recollecting every fallen or lost Warrior since the day they came into being. He relentlessly punished himself as every battle passed through his mind, every mission, and every fallen comrade.

I've accounted for every Warrior Horse, whether fallen or enslaved by the enemy. Who is Malum? His body stiffened like a corpse as he lost himself in his battles.

"Iyon?"

Caught off guard, Iyon snorted and reared around as if in one of his battles. With eyes glowing, he released a pulsating force of electric energy. Jared rolled out of the line of fire, the bolt nicking the edge of his shirt. "Iyon, stop! It's just me!"

Iyon came to and snapped at Jared, "You should know better by now than to come up behind me like that. I won't be responsible if you get killed one of these days."

Jared stood, patted the dirt off his white cuffed shirt and shrugged at the critical response. "It's good to see you too, Iyon. Why are you not down celebrating? You never let yourself do that anymore. It would be good for the people to see you there."

Iyon turned his gaze toward the village, now sounding more like a buzzing young city, and stared emotionlessly at it.

"Take in the victories we get. I don't have to be the one to tell you that. What's eating you?" Jared insisted.

Iyon snapped back; something out of character for him. "Who do you think? It's Malum. Who is he; from which descendent of our breed is he? I have spent hours recollecting all past accounts. The job of General was passed down to me from my father. He never missed a single Warrior's whereabouts. And now I have."

"So that's what this is about? You think you have failed him? Somewhere out there this Warrior was forgotten and it's eating you up that you can't give an account for him."

Iyon snorted at Jared, and glared at him. Jared gave a weary glance at his lifelong comrade and friend. For the first time since they had been in service together, Jared was concerned at the growing maliciousness that stemmed from Iyon. Jared slowly reached for his own weapon, readying himself, and stepped away. Both stared at the other, with eyes locked and waiting. Jared took care choosing his words.

"You remember all those times I stepped out of line and you whipped me around to straighten me out? That can go both ways if it needs to, my friend. This is carrying you away. I say we head to Hope, and finish this there."

"Or not."

Jared's eyes narrowed and assumed a fighting stance.

Iyon snorted and stood down. "You can stand down, Jared. I am just venting."

Iyon, it was Jen, calling out to him through her mind.

"Either way, your 'whipping' me around will have to wait. Jen is looking for me. So perhaps next time, my friend." He turned and bolted into the sky, leaving Jared in his fighting position.

Jared, feeling more relieved, loosened up and yelled out to him, "You don't think I could straighten you out? I could if I had to!"

"Of course you could!" he called back.

Jared stared at the fearless General as he flew into the city. "Now what was that all about?"

He began his long walk back toward the temple feeling that Hope should be notified of what was going on with Iyon.

Chapter 6
Into the Abyss

Iyon wandered through the crowd, searching for Jen, but couldn't find her anywhere. Many came up to him and he nodded his head and greeted them. Music filled the night air and dancing filled the street. They danced around Iyon as he walked among them, but he sensed that Jen was not among them. Looking up at the temple, he decided to see if she was there. God-given night luminaries lit up the evening sky and guided Iyon as he trotted up the stone path that led to the temple. He slowed and stepped off the path so he wouldn't make any noise. Iyon approached the bushes that surrounded much of the temple and peered through them. There was Jen, standing near the edge of the circle in the temple. She was dressed in a military uniform that was fashioned especially for women warriors. Her shoulders were pushed back, and her hands were clasped behind her. She was no longer a timid school girl, but a valiant soldier.

"You can come out of the bushes, Iyon. I know it's you," Jen said in a tone happy that he was there.

Iyon snorted and walked out into the center of the stone circle. Jen turned and stared into his eyes, raised her hand and stroked his forehead.

"Will you be coming with me, Iyon, or do you plan on missing the action?"

It hadn't even been a full twelve hours since their return, and Jen was ready to leave. Iyon wouldn't admit it out loud, but he was very proud of who she had become.

"I will be joining you," he said, his voice reflecting determination of a sure victory.

"We have the ability to rescue him now. It's time to find my father."

"They may be expecting us," he warned.

"Or maybe not. It's only been half a day. Chances are word has not gotten to them yet."

Challenging her determination, Iyon added, "When he does find out, Felonious will undoubtedly wage war against us. Are you ready for that?"

"I'll face whatever and whomever I have to in order to get my father back. And then together, we'll find my mother."

"Then you're ready. Let's go."

Jen smiled at her trusted friend. Iyon struck the center of the temple floor. It lowered and the two vanished.

Chapter 7
Decisions

The clash of thunder and lightning ignited the rocks on fire. They slid from their mound, off the cliff and avalanched down the side. Malum's black mane flapped wildly against the wind as he looked with favor at the destructive sight. Tor was hovering close by. The vortex had agreed to work with Malum in exchange for the one thing it could not give itself; freedom.

The day Iyon broke free from the Warrior's prison and defeated Queen Celesta, Malum escaped to the underground where the vortex had remained trapped for many centuries. He corroborated with the vortex and persuaded it that the witch had always known how to free it, but didn't want to, for her own selfish purposes. Feeling betrayed, Tor left Celesta to face her doom with Iyon.

Malum performed a very ancient and dark incantation he had learned from his home world. The stalagmites and stalactites had pulsated and shook with great violence until they exploded into fine particles of dust, freeing the vortex. Malum gained a strong ally that day that was willing to partake in his treacherous schemes of spreading chaos and destruction wherever he pleased. The vortex had transferred them out of the realms of Earth, where Hope could not find them. It was a world of shame, treachery, and witchcraft; a world Malum had learned to call home. This is the place where the unlikely pair plotted on how to deal with Iyon.

"Our first priority, Tor, is to take out Iyon. His presence will only hinder us. He must be captured," Malum fumed.

No. Our first priority is to no longer call me by that traitorous rat's name I let her give me. From now until forever, those who mention that name will be destroyed or exiled. This is what the vortex wanted to say, but he thought it instead. It had a name, but why give its identity to Malum? Instead, it kept its thoughts to itself, for now.

"Tor?"

The vortex spun wildly, massive clouds both gray and black swirled within as it thought of what havoc it could bring upon the worlds. Then it finally came back from its daydreaming.

"What of Jen and the River Chest?" Tor questioned.

"Jen is young and foolish. It will be impossible for her to learn the secrets of the Chest and what power she can possess from it in time, but nonetheless, it is a grave threat. If we move fast to capture Iyon, it will weaken Jen's will. She will fall easily after that. I am sure of it."

"If it's Iyon you want first, then tell me your plan, for I have never been able to breach the walls of magic that hide and protect the hidden city where Hope resides. Its source of power is far older than I."

"Iyon always travels from the city. We'll wait until he makes a move, and when he does, we'll be ready."

Another bolt of lightning ended Malum's sentence. The two agreed; the very next target would be removing Iyon, permanently.

. . . .

The constant screams that came from John pleased the Skeign, but he knew it was not enough; John's death would come before he broke, and his death was coming quickly. The beast relented from his attacks, watched John catch his breath, and then spoke to him in a cold and chilling tone.

"Your strength is mentionable, human, and I have had my fun with you, but Master demands answers. Perhaps if you won't break, we can find another to torment. Adriana, that is her name, isn't it? And yes, we have her. She is a lovely little thing. It will be our pleasure to slowly rip her to pieces unless you give me what I want." It laughed evilly.

No! How could they know? I've surrendered nothing! John's heart depleted in an instant. He could take the anguish and pain to his death, but the thought of Adriana enduring this torture broke down John's mental defense. That was all the tormentor needed and John cried out in defeat. Just then, another interrogator opened the cell door and peered in.

"Dangor, Master demands a report," it growled.

Grimacing and feeling triumphant, Dangor replied, "Tell him that I am now in the man's mind. His defenses are broken."

"Good. He will be pleased. It is time. I will send for him."

....

Jen and Iyon were lowered by the magical floating platform down into the abyss. The darkness was pierced as the light from within the floating tree illuminated the cavernous pit. Not far from the floating tree, resting on its own platform was the River Chest. The key was resting in the keyhole. As soon as Jen laid eyes on it, a rush like a mighty river swept through her. She closed her eyes as her body was swayed by the heat and the energy that had now become a part of her.

"Jen?" Iyon spoke quietly as if to gently break Jen away from it.

"Yes," she stuttered. "I'm here."

"Do not speak up during this meeting with Hope. This will be something that will have to come from me."

All right, she spoke from her soul. It was a new anomaly that Jen had discovered she could now do with Iyon, ever since her encounter with the River Chest.

Speaking soul to soul; who would've thought?

Iyon snorted, *you are a babe with all of this, Jen. You will need to traverse warily until you can be trained.*

Hope's strong and luminous glow now filled the entire room. It was powerful, more so than usual; like a fierce militant force that could not be swayed. Iyon's eyes glowed as he chose to speak soul to soul with Hope, expressing his intentions and plans, and held nothing back from her. He then stood quietly and waited for her to respond.

Waves of dark yellow expressed her deep dissatisfaction, and frustration emanated from her.

"This is reckless, Iyon. Jen has just begun her journey and has not yet started any training. She knows very little of what it means to be a Key Holder. This is both foolish and dangerous."

Iyon looked down toward the ground. Jen stood by his side, wanting so badly to speak out and defend him.

Iyon knew that Hope was right. Throwing around such power when Jen was naïve was against his better judgment, but he had weighed the options and the consequences. There was no other way.

"You know as well as I that John will not last there. We both know if they obtain what they need from him; it will bring us sure defeat. It must be done. They will expect you to wait longer, and so they will not anticipate us so soon. This gives us an upper hand and should only take a few minutes. Besides, there is no other alternative."

Hope remained silent for a moment, and then with shades of deep and sorrowful yellow, she spoke. "You are putting me in a difficult position, Iyon. I know the outcome of this. I see you, Iyon. I see your heart, your intentions. If I refuse, I can see that you will choose to disobey. Then I will be forced to carry out the law against both of you, and we cannot afford to lose you."

Humbled by her correction, he bowed in submission.

"I have always faithfully served you. As my father before me pledged loyalty to you, so have I; I will not bring shame down upon his name. Permit us to go. I will accept what comes my way while I am there."

"The gem cannot protect your presence. If you're prepared for the consequences of a battle against an army by yourself, then so be it. Do what you feel you must," Hope declared.

"Thank you." He turned to Jen. "Finding your father once we're there will be the easiest part; it's getting us back if we're under fire that will be the challenge. We will have to move fast. Speed will be our best defense."

Jen stared intently into his eyes. They were always strong and bold, but Jen could look beyond that now. She could see deeper than ever before as their gazes locked. Jen could not help herself. A part of her seemed to pass through his eyes. She began following a wild blue and silvery river that careened on and on and she became powerless in the current. She let herself be carried by the torrent and then began to see images, symbols of what could only be Iyon's emotion, anguish, pain and fear.

She was ready to surge deeper when a mighty wind appeared and swept her right out of the current. She was thrust back out of what could only be described as the depth of Iyon's soul. It was Hope who broke the silence.

"Do you know what it was you were doing?"

"No," Jen sheepishly admitted, yet shocked that the occurrence had even taken place.

"It is a forbidden thing."

Jen was overwhelmed with feelings. It wasn't emotion due to remorse at whatever she had just done. It welled up instead at the possibility of not rescuing her father and losing him to the Skeign. That's what tore at the core of her heart.

"I'm sorry. I won't do that again, but I know I can rescue him, so please let me do this. I'm asking you to trust me. I will bring him back."

"Then let it be done quickly," Hope retorted.

Iyon turned his head toward Jen standing next to him. She in return put one hand on the gem that rested at the center of Iyon's golden breastplate. She raised her other hand in the air until she was reaching straight out. The River surged through her body and poured through her outstretched arm. Jen almost fell back as the power left. Iyon shot her a nervous glance.

"Stand strong, Jen."

While the portal was forming, Jen quickly spoke her plan to Iyon. "The second we arrive there, I will disappear from you. I'll check that my father is alone. If he is, I will grab him and return to you at once."

"Then here we go."

The two jumped toward the vortex and were gone in an instant as the portal quickly shrank and vanished from existence. Within the River Chest came what sounded like the beating of a strong and vibrant heart; one that had been in existence before the birth of time.

"This will not end well, my old friend," Hope spoke to the Chest, then said nothing more; but waited intently for their return.

Chapter 8

Into the Dungeon

Innocence and playful memories filled John's mind as he and the beast walked among these thoughts. Leaning against a wired fence, John looked on with delight at his first-league baseball game. At 10 years of age, he looked out in the field and saw a short, scrawny boy as he walked cautiously up to the plate and got into ready position. John gazed at his younger self and thought how easy life had been back then.

A tight chain wrapped around John's neck jerked him away from the fence. It pulled him close to the beast so that his blackened mane rubbed against John's face, and then John was thrown to the ground. As he landed on his back, a giant paw with jagged flesh-ripping claws pressed down upon his chest.

"Using old memories to protect that which you try so hard to hide; a bold but futile attempt, human. I have done this for centuries; there is no use for this game. Nonetheless, I will find what I need," Dangor growled.

Immediately the baseball field slipped away and all of John's boyhood memories were scanned, but nothing was hidden or seemed extraordinary. Then, moving into John's teenage and college years, every memory was probed. From classrooms to games, going out with friends, and his marriage, every detail was clear and ordinary. In disgust, Dangor could not find what he was looking for. Impatience fueled his anger. It jerked John toward him and shook him violently by the chain.

"Enough! Show me what I need or I will leave you right now. I will drag Adriana into a cell and make her suffer far worse than you. You will hear her screams, and there will be no way to save her."

That did it. John had no strength to fight any longer, so he surrendered his will. He was broken, worn, and defenseless. John took the beast to the library. It was the first day he had ever laid eyes on Adriana. The beast gave John another annoyed shake for the trouble he had caused. Adriana was sitting at her usual table stacked full of books, quietly working. Dangor looked up and toward the back of the library. There was an oddly decorated wooden door which John had tried to mask in his mind, making it to appear ordinary. But the memories behind them were so real and magical that it had changed the content of the door itself. It was now transformed. Beautiful figurines created out of gold bulged right out of the door's wooden framework.

Dangor grinned, and marched John toward the door.

"Open it!"

Tears streamed down John's face as he wrapped his hand around the golden knob.

I'm sorry! I'm so sorry, Tolare. I have failed you! I have failed us all...

The door opened.

. . . .

Jen and Iyon traveled through the portal and ended exactly where Jen last saw her father. She turned and gasped at what was left of it. Nothing but a blackened charred mess remained of the tall tree stump that had been there before.

What has my father done?

"Jen, quick. We have no time for lamenting. Find your father, but let me know what your plan is before you execute anything. Hurry! Leave now."

Without responding, she vanished. Iyon stood motionless. Falling into a deep meditation, he cast his presence deep into the recess of the gem he wore upon his neck in hopes to shield his presence the best he could. Now all Jen had to do was hurry.

. . . .

Jen reappeared in the dungeon cell where her father was being held. The sight appalled her, filled her with rage, anguish and malice. There, trapped in a torturous tomb came the whimpering screams and panting of her dying father. The sounds stuck knives into her heart. She cursed herself for not getting there sooner. The Skeign was also there; his tentacle was hidden down a tube-shaped shaft that led into the tomb-like cocoon her father was entrapped in. Jen looked directly at the gruesome creature but the eyes were blackened over as if incased in oil. It did not see Jen standing there, for it was lost inside of John's mind. Then it let out a horrendous laugh.

. . . .

The piercing of a red laser, as hard as a sharpened sword, slashed Iyon across the neck, throwing him on his side. Not only did Iyon's mental concentration break, blood oozed out of the wound, and burned hotter than fire. He neighed wildly from the burning torture. Malum had returned to collect him, and Iyon was caught off guard. Iyon ignored the immense pain; his life depended on it. He jumped to his feet. With power blazing from his soul, he returned fire toward his enemy. Malum counterattacked with another blast of his own, causing an explosion between them. Then both finally stopped and squared off toward one another. Malum laughed wickedly at the sight of Iyon's wound.

"I'm not going to waste my time talking to you here, Iyon. You're coming with us!"

Us? Iyon's ears flattened.

Malum snickered as the vortex appeared directly behind Iyon, positioning him between two enemies. Desperate to break up the vortex's stability, he lurched back and fired a massive burst of light energy at the side of the vortex, causing it to slide backward and break up.

"Enough games! You have no hope of defeating us," Malum's snarled command was vicious. Iyon attacked Malum with all his strength as the vortex regained its power and drew nearer from behind. In a few seconds, Iyon knew he would become their prisoner. But then the roar of a thousand monsters stopped Malum's attack. The two Warrior Horses looked up.

From all sides, the hilltops surrounding the valley were covered with the Skeign army as they peered down at the intruders. Hundreds of Skeign leaped into the air and others came at full stride from all directions. The sky filled with thousands of crimson lasers as the beasts hungrily sought to kill their wretched foes once and for all. The vortex tried to scoop Iyon up, but he stepped out of its path while taking vicious hits from the Skeign. Malum scowled in disgust as his body was pelted from the surrounding enemy. Malum jumped into the vortex which then disappeared from sight, leaving Iyon alone to face an entire army of his hated enemy. The gem glared all shades of glory as Iyon reached for every source of its strength. He would destroy the army if he had to. With an uncanny sense for vengeance, Iyon created a sphere of power that circled around him, and then cast it in all directions. It mercilessly cut through the first wave of the Skeign. Their bodies fell limp and lifeless to the ground.

That attack from Iyon did not scare these black creatures of the night off. This made them want to rip Iyon apart even more with their razor sharp claws. These monstrous lion creatures with wings leaped over the dead and continued to pour down from all the hilltops. With all their might they charged at their foe, hoping to overpower him and avenge the blood of their fallen comrades.

Iyon became a machine of death as the warrior in him rose and took over. He stood his ground and continuously destroyed wave after wave of those who dared to advance against him. Iyon's entire coat of fur became stained with blood from his wounds, but he would not stop; he could not!

. . . .

Rage filled Jen at the grotesque sight. She could not take it another second. Reaching for the river of power that secretly surged within her, she held up her hand and within a second, a vortex was created. The Skeign never knew what hit it. It released John a second before its doom and glared at Jen with widened eyes full of shock and hatred. She thrust the vortex at it, swallowing it whole, and sending it to an unknown abyss. Dangor was gone and with it, all the secrets it had drawn out of John.

Jen ran to the tomb and unlatched the clamps. The cocoon exploded open as the surge of fresher air pushed the lid open and there she beheld her dying father. In just a matter of days, his body had dissolved to skin and bones. The stone tablet was drenched in his blood from his shackled wrists and ankles. She unstrapped the helmet and gently pulled it off her father's limp head.

A parade of footsteps sounded down the hall.

Jen unclasped her father's hands and ankles and gently raised him to her chest.

The cell door burst open and there, standing in the doorway was a man, crimson eyes full of malice and darkened hair flowing down past his shoulders. Overwhelming energy poured from him toward Jen. Jen stared at the beautiful evil for only a moment, not knowing who or what he was. She thought of Iyon and vanished from his sight, taking John with her.

. . . .

Jen and her father landed with a splash. The mounting piles of dead Skeign creatures had created an arena around them, quickly filling with blood of the dead. Flashes of light energy filled the sky along with howls and torturous screams. The Skeign climbed over the masses of the fallen from all directions around Iyon. They leaped madly toward him in hopes that they could find vengeance for all he had destroyed. But each and every one met their fate.

The Warrior Horse was covered in deep gashes across his entire body. His blood poured from his wounds and mixed with the lake of blood that flowed from his enemies. Even though Iyon knew he was closer to death then he had ever been before, he refused to show any sign of it. He fought on. He would kill them all if he could. The Skeign growled horrifically at their humiliating failure.

"Iyon!" was all Jen could say, horrified at the sight of his wounds.

"Waste no time!" he desperately panted.

The Skeign made one last futile attempt to leap toward him from all directions. Flashes of lightning power surged at them. Iyon blocked the blasts that would have hit Jen and her father as the vortex was being created and scooped them from that ghastly planet, leaving the mass of bodies and blood for their Master to see. Liel would surely mourn this great defeat.

Chapter 9
Unspoken

The vortex set the three of them directly on the mystical floating stone, as soft as a padded cushion. It hardened after they had landed on it. They were in the presence of the giant tree. Hope's glow filled the cavern. Iyon's body fell lifelessly to the ground. Jen was still clutching to her father. She laid his head down and threw herself onto Iyon. His eyes were no longer blue and vibrant, but black and sunken in. Another stone floated nearby. Jared, Fox, Azar, and Jeremiah were there; two of them carried a cot to rest John on.

Jen remembered what she had done for Zurina and hoped beyond all hope that she could do the same for Iyon. Her face was streaked with tears as she placed her palm over the largest gash on Iyon's neck and let power flow through her and down into Iyon's body. Some of the smaller gashes began to close up, and then something happened to Jen. The flow of power stopped. Her body flushed as if her entire life source was drained from her. She paled instantly. It was Hope that had stopped her. If she had gone another second, Jen would have surely died.

"I'm so sorry, my friend," was all she could say, and pulled herself off his body. Jared and Fox lifted John onto the cot and stepped back onto the other stone.

It was Azar who broke the sullen silence. "Jen, you must come with us. These wounds go far deeper than what can be seen. Iyon has to be left here.

Hope is the only one to save him now." Azar pulled her up and clasped one arm around her as she listlessly stumbled onto the other floating platform. It quickly rose until they were above ground and in the center of the outer temple. Jen felt as if Iyon was now sealed in a hollow grave.

Iyon, can you hear me?....Get well, my friend.

There was no response from the stallion. All Jen could feel was darkness, great remorse and irreparable loss. Dazed and lost in sadness, she followed the procession that led to Dahlia's cabin among the fields of Tolare.

Over the next few days, very few words were spoken in Dahlia's cabin. Jen remained by her father's side as he rested in his bed day and night. The only time she left was when Dahlia came in with nurses to clean and dress John's wounds and nourish him with their herbs and medicines. Every time the door closed on her, she would cringe, hating every moment she had to be away from her father.

Finally John began to stir during the early morning hours of the third day as Jen was dozing by his bedside. Jen's body flinched from the sound of him stirring and leaned closer to the bed.

She was about to call Dahlia's name, but then stopped short. She wanted to savor this moment alone with her father. She leaned closer to him and gently cupped his bandaged hand in hers.

"Dad," she gently whispered. Streams of uncontrollable tears stained her face.

He swayed his head to the left and then to the right, as if he was trying to pull himself out of his own reverie. Slowly, his eyes opened as he emerged from his continuous sleep. He caught Jen's image and stared in a daze of disbelief at her, his eyes sunken and sad.

"I wish you were really here with me," he faintly spoke.

"It's no dream, Dad," she said gently. "You are here in Tolare with me. You're safe with me now. Dahlia is here too. She has been taking good care of you. It's over."

John's sadness did not lift as Jen had hoped it would.

John turned his head away and the expression on his face seemed to reflect shame and remorse. Confused and dismayed, Jen got up and fetched

Dahlia, who was in the kitchen, preparing the soup. She looked toward Jen, "My dear, what can I do for you?"

"My father has awoken."

Jen's face was cast down toward the ground. She then sat at the table and let out a loud disappointed sigh. She was hoping for a different response from him, but given what John had just been through, what could she expect from him?

Dahlia scooped some soup in a bowl, grabbed a wooden spoon and brought it over to Jen. She knew exactly what turmoil was going on within Jen. "I see you, my dear. Your father will recover, but he is not the same father you remember from your former life. Learn to understand and accept who he has become. There aren't too many who have gone through what he has, and lived to tell the tale. Your father will need some time to recover. In the meantime, take time for yourself. Explore Tolare, and all she has to offer. It is a wondrous place and there is more to it than you can imagine. And no matter where you wander off to, you will be safe, for there is no evil or Skeign to chase after you here." With that, Dahlia grabbed another bowl of soup and spoon, and headed toward John's room. "Take the day, Jen. I'll see you tonight for supper."

The thought of exploration lightened her spirits. And it was true, Jen had not had the time to meander and explore any of Tolare since she had been there. In a sense, the idea of doing so made her feel half normal again. Knowing that her father was going to be okay gave her a sense of relief for the first time in months.

She devoured the soup, washed her dish and spoon in the basin and put them away in the cabinet.

Heading outside the cabin, Jen noticed a trail leading to the woods. Jen headed in that direction, thinking she would prefer the solitude of the woods over the bustling young city. A brief interlude of peace for her had finally come.

Chapter 10
A Perfect Day

Jen roamed the rolling hills until she reached the edge of the Tolarian Forest. The temperature outside was always perfect, along with the breeze. She turned and looked back at the little city. Smoke rose peacefully from rooftops and festive music floated on the air. Tolare's playful setting made it a true utopia compared to the nightmare that raged all around them.

Who would ever want to leave this perfect place?

Excited for the break for exploration, Jen turned and wandered into the forest. Every tree stood proud and tall as it magnificently illuminated deep shades of green and peculiarly shaped leaves. Iridescent flowers blanketed the floor of the forest along with exotic bushes full of luscious berries. Jen meandered down the trail through the green wonderland as the sounds of animal life and chirping birds filled the air. She breathed in the delicate aroma of the forest flowers and felt the forest's peace and harmony.

I wish Mom were here to see this.

During that moment of quiet tranquility, laughter rang out; childlike laughter. She smirked and picked up her pace to see if she could find the source. Before long she was hurdling over moss-covered logs and running through patches of ferns, looking in all directions. She listened and heard it again, that enticing burst of laughter.

Jen stopped and grimaced at her oversight for not looking up into the trees sooner. The laughter came from somewhere far above her. Some of the trees in the forest extended hundreds of feet in the air. Jen didn't care how silly it seemed; she wanted to discover who it was that could hide so well among the canopy of the trees. With self-determination, Jen selected a shorter tree with branches she could reach and started her climb. As she got higher up, she saw how the branches of many trees intertwined with one another, making a dangerous upwards path if one dared to climb. She looked for ways to go higher and higher and switched from tree to tree as the branches interlocked. With amazing ease, she walked on many small branches, perfectly poised and unfaltering. The inner balance was a pleasant surprise to Jen. She was completely in tune with the forest.

After an hour of careful climbing, Jen reached the top branch of one of the tallest trees she had ever seen. She walked on it toward the trunk. Other branches circled the trunk like a staircase, inviting her to the very top of the canopy.

"Hey," called a boy's voice.

She looked straight ahead. There was a rustle against the branches as a boy leaped down and jumped directly onto her branch. There she was, standing face to face with a fellow; only slightly taller than her, brown uncut hair and wild carefree eyes to match. His muscular tone made his age hard to determine. Jen stared in confidence at the boy, feeling proud and completely unafraid.

The old Jen would've startled…probably fallen too, she thought to herself as she laughed on the inside.

Tilting his head only slightly, he said, "Impressive climbing skills; most people don't have the will to make it even halfway up."

"I'm not one to give up easily."

"Also impressive. Well, come on then. Follow me and I'll introduce you to the others."

Feeling free-spirited for the first time since she lost her father, Jen smiled and followed him as he jumped from branch to branch. The branches wound their way around the trunk all the way up to the top. But hidden in the canopy was not something that Jen would have ever expected. The stair-like branches led through the thick leaves straight into a platform of a man-made structure surrounded on all sides by nature's flawless camouflage. It was perfectly concealed and not visible for any to see from the ground below. There was no roof except for the top branches that twisted upwards, creating some protection from the light of the day. And there, among wooden chairs and beds of leaves, were a few older boys she was about to meet.

As soon as they entered, the carefree boy who brought her there spoke, "Look who made her way up here."

When the group looked at Jen, she saw expressions of carefree living and acceptance on their faces. She could feel that they were nonjudgmental of her. It was the first time Jen could remember that she was welcomed. It was a good feeling.

"Hey," they all said in quick succession. Jen took in the appearance of all of them. There were just three others dressed for true Tolarian adventure. She thought they could be teenagers, but their bodies were built for war; each one of them in extremely good condition. All of them had the same expression in their eyes. Yes, she could see that they were happy, yet she could also tell that they hid secrets.

"Hey, name's Jen," was all she could think of to say.

She wasn't sure if she could come out and say that she was the daughter of John. Jen wanted to be known just as Jen that day.

"My name is Micol," said the one who'd led her there. He turned toward his friends and introduced them. "That's Jendal, Shek, and Brendin."

Jen nodded to them all, and then looked at their tree. "So, do you live up here?"

"Yeah, this is our home," Micol answered. He reached in a basket and pulled out a jug of water and handed it to Jen. By now, her throat was parched and dry from the climb, but she refused to show any sign of weakness in front of them. Still, there was no way that she could pass up a chance to quench her thirst. So she gratefully took it and drank.

"We're all that are left of our families. When Iyon brought us to Tolare, we tried living among the people, but it wasn't working for us. So we moved out here."

"And no one said anything?" Jen questioned them, feeling out their motives. She looked into Micol's eyes. For a moment, she felt she had the ability to look past his eyes and tour the motives of his heart and soul. She knew she could, but what would that do to him and how would that make him feel? Why could she suddenly have the newfound power to do this, but was told that it was forbidden by Hope? Or maybe, it just wasn't understood by them. Jen fought her feelings and held back as Micol continued to talk; completely unaware of what Jen was tempted to do.

"No, not during these times. Most our age are…training for things they are told to learn. We…well, we found our peace here. No one minds since we don't cause any trouble."

Found your peace, or hiding in its shadows? And that's when she felt it, emanating from everyone around her. All at once, Jen could see things in a different light, a power she knew came from the River Chest. Whether light or darkness, she could feel it. The sensation of such an experience overwhelmed her. She quickly looked away and rubbed her eyes; acting like something was in them as she wiped a tear away. The sudden desire to find Iyon and talk to him pressed on her. These changes that were going on within her left her confounded and guarded. What was she becoming?

"I should probably go." Feeling odd, she turned to leave.

"Where to?" asked Micol.

"I don't know, back to Tolare, I guess."

"This is all Tolare. There's more to see, you know, even beyond the woods."

"How could that be? The underground can't go on for that long without being discovered by the Skeign."

"Because," Micol said with a smile and he raised his hands, "It is Tolare! Have you seen the army yet?"

"Micol!" yelled his friends.

"Have you been to the training fields?" Micol persisted.

"I didn't even know there were training fields. And no, I haven't seen the army."

"Then it's time to see the other half. Come on, I'll take you."

The others stared at him grimly. Brendin was the tallest of the group and now their spokesman. "That's not a good idea, Micol." The others clearly agreed. Jen could tell that they were from the camp. It was also evident that they did not want to return or be found.

"It's ok, Micol," Jen interrupted, not wanting her new friends to quarrel on account of her. But then there was that side of her that wanted the adventure. In essence, Jen hungered for the journey, and the curiosity of an entire army she never knew Tolare had was too enticing for her; so she changed her mind on what she was going to say to him. "If you know how to be careful and watch your back, then I say let's do it."

Micol looked at Brendin, who was opposing him and nonchalantly said, "It'll be fine. Their scouting practices will be done hours before we get there and I won't get too close. Besides, there's no way they can sneak up on me. So, Jen, you ready?"

Brendin could tell there was no way of talking Micol out of this, so he consented, "You know the code, man."

"Yes, I know the code, Brendin. Besides, I'd never give this place away. This is our place."

"And what about the girl?" he asked, turning his attention and concern to Jen.

She held up her hands in quick surrender. "I only met Micol, I never saw any of you," she responded with an assuring smile.

Brendin clasped hands with Micol and said, "Watch your back, man."

"I gotchu."

As the two headed down, the group of trusted friends called out to them and gave their warnings to be careful.

Over the next couple hours, Jen followed her navigator through the intertwining branches that formed magical pathways hundreds of feet above the ground. Throughout the entire trip, Micol talked of his old home, what things were like before the day the Skeign attacked, and how grateful they were to be rescued. He talked on and on as the day passed, but as they drew to the forest's end, they traveled in silence. By twilight, they reached the edge of the forest, the whole time being able to stay far above the ground.

There, Jen gazed at the mass of the army, thousands strong spread out before them. The first thing she looked for were swords, sparring and fighting, but this was no typical army. There were shooting ranges as many took turns with the weapons Jen had seen and used herself in Shadow Earth. There were dozens of tents with tables surrounded by masses of people as they worked to build and fashion weapons. This was a different side of Tolare. This side was preparing for war.

The Tolarian sun was setting, and the sights of the camp were becoming hard to see. Jen saw campfires lit in between the army tents. She could tell from the sweet aromas that rose from the camp that dinner was well on its way. Her stomach growled in retaliation for all the climbing she had been doing.

Jen glanced at Micol, and saw the look in his eyes as he circled and stared deep through all the trees and surveyed the ground. Feeling safe that the scouts had long since retreated for the day, he turned his attention to the camp and blissfully stared. His face appeared blank, and for a moment, Micol seemed mysteriously elusive.

"I wanted you to see this. Iyon built this army up from nothing. It's quite a sight, isn't it?" he said, his voice filled with a sad wonder.

"It is a sight. It's hard to believe Iyon began all this. Where I'm from," Jen almost trailed off on how he would be nothing more than a horse, but caught herself just in time. "Well, he's a legend."

"I don't know how much good an army could do against a million Skeign, but the people feel that it's a hope for a future, one they didn't have before. We should go now. I'm not in much of a mood to run into the army right now, and I know you're hungry. When we get further into the woods, I have some reserves hidden away in the trees, so we'll be fine for food."

Micol held up his hand, signaling for her to be silent, and tensed up like a rock. They were being watched, and he had noticed far too late. Two soldiers dropped down on either side of Jen and Micol, and others came out from their hiding spots. Micol's hands formed fists, but then loosened as he relaxed, confident that he could escape from them at a better time.

"Micol," said the lead soldier. With weapon in hand, his voice sounded tense from having to face Micol.

Micol didn't flinch, but continued to stare at the camp.

"It's well past scouting hours; you boys aren't usually out this late," Micol said in obvious dismay.

"Normally we aren't, but since a young girl of high interest was reported missing, we were told to scout longer. Didn't expect to run into you though. You've been quite evasive as of late."

"It's one of my strengths."

"Not today, apparently," the soldier said.

"No," Micol said with great intimidation. "Not today."

Then the soldier turned his attention to Jen, not knowing if it was her or not. "Speak honestly ma'am; are you Jen, the daughter of John? We've been looking all over for her and you fit the description."

"Yes, sir," was all Jen could muster up.

"Then you need to come with us. You both will be taken to camp," the soldier eyed Micol while pulling out hand restraints, "Micol, I'll need your hands, slowly." Weapons were raised and pointed at both of them.

Micol glared at the soldier, tensed and ready to fight. The sensations Jen was feeling from them left her unnerved and she retaliated, "Is that really necessary?"

Micol wanted so badly to give them a quick lesson in how fierce and evasive he could be, but with Jen right there and now knowing who she really was, he felt perplexed and caught off guard; so he reluctantly put his hands in front of him and the soldier quickly fastened the restraints around them. In the back of his mind, Micol wasn't worried about the restraints. He knew exactly what to do and as soon as they headed down the ropes, he would plan to make his escape. But then a key was turned and removed from the restraints and they began to glow a florescent blue.

"What's this?" Micol remarked in shocked disappointment.

"It's new. Iyon is having them installed now. Ever since the last incident, thanks to you, we realized we needed to take better measures. And only Iyon himself can command them to depower. And the great thing about these is any further retaliation while wearing this leads to instant immobilization, my friend. So that's end game for tonight, Micol."

The lead soldier signaled the others and within seconds they were surrounded on the massive branches of the giant Tolarian trees. Over the course of two minutes they had attached harnesses on Jen and Micol and in a few more minutes, the company was on the ground. With Jen and Micol in the middle of a circle of them, they made their way into camp; all the while, keeping a close eye on Micol's every move.

The group walked toward the center of the army camp until they came upon a group of tables overseen by Fox. Fox looked up at the group, and grimaced as the soldiers stepped aside to expose the two they were escorting. Fox stood tall and strong, and placing his hands behind his back, he glared at the two of them.

"Out of all of Tolare! I should've known you two would somehow find each other, but I would dare say fate brought you to me…Micol, it's been awhile."

Micol stood militantly, his gaze fixed straight forward. "Hello, sir. Good as always to see you, too." The rebellion in his tone was more than obvious.

Fox turned his attention to Jen. "We're very surprised to see you here. There are more than a few people wondering where you went off to."

"Dahlia said it was okay," Jen said in her own defense.

"Mm hmm. A couple of hours into town, Jen; but being John's daughter, Dahlia should've guessed that would've led to some uncanny adventure. You also found the only trouble that Tolare has, and you did it all in one day. Imagine the odds," he finished while shaking his head.

Micol made a slight noise in his throat, but didn't budge or look at Jen. He didn't have to; Jen could feel his stare even if she were a mile away from him. A rush of confusion and frustration fused her being. Why should she feel guilty? It was apparent that he wasn't honest with her to begin with. Then again, neither was she, and now he was in trouble because of it. The whole situation left a sour taste in her mouth, and certainly left little room for handling another scolding from Fox. Either way, Jen did her best to smile and lighten the mood.

"Scolding me again, Fox?" she chimed.

Fox tilted his head toward her. "I guess it's becoming a habit of mine. Well, enough of this for tonight. I'll see to it that you two get a proper meal. I guarantee it'll be a better meal than wild berries from the forest that he had in store for you. Come with me."

Surrounded by the guards, the two followed Fox to the center of camp. The wave of whispers among the young men and women spread like wildfire throughout the camp. For everyone knew who Micol was and what he was known for. Jen burned with curiosity at who this boy could be or what he had done. Who was she walking next to? What past did he have in order to cause this kind of stir? She noticed that he paid no attention to them as they walked on. His eyes remained strong, fearless and steady. Qualities she found dangerously attractive.

He's seasoned with this. That much, Jen knew for sure, but no way would she push him for the story; that would be something she wanted him to tell on his own accord.

They finally reached the center of the camp. Fox directed Jen to a large tent that could hold thirty or more people. A woman came out and stood in front of them.

Jen smiled ear to ear.

With a weapon strapped on her side, her long hair pulled back, and wearing militant clothes, was Zurina.

"Zurina?" Jen asked in amazement, barely believing her eyes yet relieved to see the face of a friend. "I thought you had stayed in town with your sister."

"You mean this sister!" yelled a young woman from somewhere within the tent. "Sorry, I can't come out to personally greet you. Zurina's got me trying to figure out how to put this stupid contraption together before I can see the light of day again! Ahh, this stupid thing!"

Zurina half-smiled and spoke quietly, "She needs to toughen up a little."

"I heard that!" retorted her sister.

Fox interrupted the brigade, "Micol, you'll be staying in this one," he pointed to the tent across from Zurina's.

Just then, Jared ran up. He was carrying a scroll in one hand, and a weapon in the other. He would've strode right past them had Fox not broken his train of thought.

"Jared," Fox called out, "You'll be having a guest in your tent tonight."

Jared stopped to see who Fox was talking about. As soon as he saw who it was, he was speechless, and after a raise of an eyebrow, directed at Micol, he disappeared into his tent.

"Well, being in the middle of the camp and under watchful eyes should make it all the harder to sneak out," Fox stated.

"Not likely." It was a sharp and sarcastic come back. Jen stared at him, stunned.

"Pardon?" Fox stepped closer until he was just a foot away.

Micol broke his straight forward glare and looked downward, trying to hold his tongue, but to little avail.

"I mean yes, sir," he said with a hint of sarcasm and raising his head to defiantly match eyes with the higher ranking officer.

Fox glared at the rebel.

"Come on in here, you two. You've got to be hungry." Zurina broke the tension. Thankful for the escape, the two stepped back from Fox and ducked away, quickly following Zurina into the tent.

Though Micol still had the restraints on, with a spoon in one hand and a piece of bread in the other, he had no problem scarfing down two bowls of the beef stew compared to Jen's one bowl. All the while, Jen sat across from him and glared at him, saying nothing. For some time, she waited for an explanation, but impatience was getting the better of her as he continued to remain silent.

"Are you going to tell me what this," pointing to the restraints, "is all about?"

"No. When were you planning on telling me who you are?" Micol asked sarcastically.

"When were you planning on telling me the same?" Jen retaliated, "And what about…"

Micol looked up and threw her a pleading look, knowing that she was about to mention the others.

She leaned closer and whispered, "Then you better promise me you'll tell me later."

"Alright, if I'm not in the barracks by morning, I will. I'm surprised I'm not there now."

Jen looked toward the tent door and saw the guards posted. Zurina sat toward the back of the tent. She nodded her head, "Probably because of them."

He looked in dismay, but then said nonchalantly, "Aye, probably so," and continued to eat.

"Micol, what did you get yourself into?" she pestered further.

"Just this and that, mostly. Much of it was just a misunderstanding, I feel."

Jen finished her soup and didn't press the issue further. At that moment, Jared came in and nodded to Jen.

"Evening, Jen."

"Good to see you again, Jared." This caused Micol to glare at Jen. Why was it that she seemed to know everyone who had it out for him?

"There's been more than just a few people worried about your whereabouts today, but I'm glad to see you are safe. I'm surprised to see you on the far side of Tolare. Not something we can say we were anticipating."

Micol looked out the corner of his eye toward Jared and remarked, "She's John's daughter. Should you have suspected anything less?"

Jen interrupted them before Micol got himself into any more trouble with his mouth. "I'm sorry, Jared. I didn't realize the forest was so big."

"Yes, that it is. Well, get some rest and we'll talk more in the morning. Micol, you're with me now," Jared said firmly.

Micol sighed, tossed an apologetic look at Jen and slowly rose. "Don't suppose these will come off?"

"No," Jared snapped. "This time I'm seeing to it that you are fully secure for the night. After you." They walked to the entrance of the tent and vanished into the night.

Zurina came up to the table and sat across from Jen. "Out of all the boys to meet in Tolare, Jen, you run into the one boy that causes the most trouble and mischief."

Jen smiled. *Is that supposed to make me feel bad?*

"Well I'm not surprised. I'll show you your cot so you can get some rest," Zurina then stood up as Jen did also.

"We need to catch up some time, Zurina. It's refreshing to see a friendly face in the midst of constant war."

"Until then, we'll have to take the small chances we get. But for tonight just rest; I can tell you need to."

Zurina pulled back a drape revealing a small space with a lamp and a cot.

"I'll see you in the morning," Zurina said as she turned to leave.

"Good night," Jen said as the drape closed her in.

Jen lay on her cot and the buzz in the camp died down to a quiet still as everyone retired to their places to sleep for the night. With a smile on her face, Jen closed her eyes, thought about her day, and how incredibly perfect it seemed to her. Reality slipped away and unconsciousness soon took over.

Chapter 11
Until then...

The dreams became a blur as Jen was nudged back into reality. When her eyes cleared, it was Iyon's form that filled her vision. Her heart flooded with a firestorm of emotions. She wrapped her arms around his neck and he bent down and wrapped his head around her as best he could. They stayed there for some time.

I'm so sorry, Iyon; I don't know why I couldn't help you.

It was not your place. It was not your fault. I went on my own accord knowing what would happen. But it is done now, and you have your father back. You were not supposed to have strayed this far. You caused Dahlia much unwarranted stress.

I'm sorry, I just...got caught up.

Yes, so I've heard, and with one that needs to be reckoned with.

He is just a boy.

Not just any boy, but Jared's brother and the son of the man who commanded the Tolarian army before the fall of Tran.

Jen pulled away and looked directly at Iyon. "You're kidding me!"

"I am not. I have let Jared make the decisions on how to handle the situation concerning his rebellious younger brother. But now that he is here, I'm taking over."

That made Jen worried.

"Clean clothes were brought in for you. Get yourself dressed and ready.

When you have eaten breakfast, come out. I should be ready by then."

Excited to have a chance to talk to Micol that morning, Jen sprang into action. After she finished her morning preparations, she walked out to meet Iyon. As Jen emerged, she looked like a Tolarian woman warrior.

Her eyes immediately found him. Micol was sitting on a log close to a morning fire. His hands, to her great dismay, were still in restraints. Jared was sitting next to him, his arms crossed; his face more the persona of a father than a brother. From what Jen could tell, the exchange of words between the two was not going well. It concluded with Micol shaking his head no. Jared sighed, got up, and walked over to where Iyon was.

"He's not going to cooperate with me," Jared spoke in a low voice.

"This is no longer your problem."

"Micol," Iyon said militantly.

Micol lifted his head and stared at Iyon, his stubbornness expressed by his blank and impassive stare. Jen could feel Iyon's tensed demeanor from where she was standing.

"Come here."

Reluctantly, Micol stood to his feet and walked slowly to Iyon, stopping a few short feet before him.

"Is it true that you chose not to cooperate with your brother? We know there are others involved."

"It is true."

"It is senseless of you to do this while knowing the consequences."

"I have enough 'consequences' on my plate. Wouldn't hurt to add on a few more."

Still a smart mouth, Jen thought.

"You betray them by leading them astray. This will be discussed no further here. Your recklessness is now my burden. You will be taken to the temple, where you will remain until a decision is made concerning you."

Micol remained silent, knowing that arguing would be completely useless.

Iyon turned his attention to Jared, "Take him through the southernmost trail; it is protected by magic, so there will be no issues with the transition."

Before Jen could say hello or goodbye, Micol was escorted away by a round of guards.

Iyon?

Iyon turned around and saw Jen standing outside of Zurina's tent, and walked over to her.

It's time for us to go. Climb on my back.

I didn't even get to talk to him. Why didn't you let me have the chance to talk to him?

I didn't know you needed to.

He was in the forest, not causing any harm. You should just let him return.

That is not your call. He needs to heal. And I don't want us to speak of this in front of the army. For now, this issue with Micol is over. Your mind is clouded. Climb on and lay this matter to rest.

Angrily, Jen straddled Iyon and he turned and took off at a quick pace. The flow of emotions rampaging through her carried with it confusion and frustration. She knew she had no right to question one that had command of an entire army, let alone hurt her friendship she had with Iyon, but still…

I'm sorry. I just…I don't know. I'll put it to rest for now. But promise me we'll talk later.

That is fine, but this is something your father will ultimately need to handle.

As soon as Iyon reached the end of camp, he broke out into a full stride, racing toward the edge of the forest. Jen clung on to his mane and leaned forward. Seconds before colliding with the trees, the ground gave way from underneath them, and then Iyon was galloping at full speed through a tunnel that ran beneath the forest.

Chapter 12
To be Decided

Adriana sat there, staring at herself in the mirror on her vanity. The bluish gems embedded in her dress dazzled in the light of her room. She was given a beautiful navy blue gown from Liel, along with other trinkets and gifts of gold and diamonds. He said it was the least he could do to ease her suffering. She put in her new diamond earrings, and she stood up and glided through the room toward the door. Before opening it to leave, she took one more look around. Her dream-like suite had everything she could've ever wanted, even her own personal pool. Despite the fact that her family was aiding the enemy, she felt quite content. Liel had taken good care of her, and she would be sure to return the favor. She opened the door and walked out where she met dozens of other people who were found and brought here by Liel to help him with his special assignments. Locking the door with a simple swipe of her hand, she walked ritually to her new designated room; her job had now changed, requiring less stress. Looking for one of their own was not as taxing. As Liel had told them all, it was now his highest priority to find the one that was called Dangor. It was a timely reprieve for Adriana, and she enjoyed it. With a new touch of elegance, she sashayed down the hall.

"Adriana," said one of the Leads that kept time and order of their schedules.

Adriana turned and gave him immediate attention and respect. "Yes, sir."

"Liel has sent orders of a different kind for you. You will not be joining the others with the Dangor assignment. Yours is a higher priority than that. You must come with me."

"Yes, sir," was her response as she filled with pride for being considered highly honored above the others.

Adriana turned and followed the Lead, disappointed that she had worn such a fine dress for a job she knew she would sweat profusely while working. She didn't want to dirty it with that smell. But if she were successful in rescuing her family, she guessed it would be worth the small sacrifice. Her boundless determination and focus set her far apart from the rest, something that Liel continually used to his benefit.

I will find you, my family. I will find you and bring you home to me, Adriana thought.

. . . .

As Iyon sprinted along the tunnel under the forest, the ground went into a steep incline and in a flash, the two emerged from a hollowed-out tree trunk somewhere near the edge of the forest, not too far from the city. It was one of the entrances and exits to the many secret passageways that lay beneath Tolare. Iyon slowed to a walk. He was panting and sweating. It was the first time Jen had ever seen him fighting for breath.

Iyon?

I'm okay. Taking you somewhere first.

Iyon walked down a tranquil path that extended off the beaten trail. It twisted and turned until it ended at the base of the widest tree Jen had ever laid her eyes on. Around the other side of the tree was an open hilly field, and then the busy city of Tolare. The roots of the tree were mostly above ground, pushing the base of the tree at least fifteen feet from the ground. The roots created a strong barrier in almost a perfect circumference besides a few breaks which could be used as oddly shaped windows. There was a triangular opening the roots made that could be used as an entrance.

"This is my home. I wanted you to see it."

Jen smiled as she looked at it, and then slid off of Iyon, letting him lead the way into his own home. After she followed him in, a light flickered on and she noticed a small glowing gem that floated near the ceiling and illuminated the entire interior.

It was a simple home, thought Jen, but then what did a horse really need? A large bed of hay, buckets of oats and a large tub filled with water colored blue and slightly glowed, because it was mixed with a medicine that he needed in order to continue healing.

Iyon groaned as he staggered over to the basin of water and began to drink it down. Seeing him this weak and frail made Jen's skin crawl; he had sacrificed a great deal for her, a debt she did not know if she could ever repay.

"Is there anything I can do? Will you let me try again, please?" Jen asked as she fought back the desire to tear up.

Iyon lifted his head from the water, but did not look in her direction. "I will be fine in a couple more days. Hope is helping me daily. But I brought you here because I have something for you."

Iyon stepped over to the massive bed of hay and kicked at it until a bag was revealed. He then bent down and pulled out John's leather bag by carefully nipping at just the strap. He turned to give it to Jen.

"My father's bag," she said with a smile beaming across her face. "I'd almost forgotten about it. I'll bring it to him right away. I can't wait to see the look on his face when he sees this! Thanks, Iyon. Are we far from Dahlia's? I know my father is resting, but I would like to see if he is ready to see me."

"Dahlia's house is just two hills over, but John isn't there. As soon as he had enough strength, he demanded a conference with Hope. It's where we're going. I am strengthened enough for now, so climb on so that we can meet with them."

After Iyon finished drinking the amount he needed to feel strengthened again; Jen climbed back on and the two left Iyon's quaint home. As soon as they were clear of the tree, Iyon jumped and took off into the sky. The two glided quietly over the city of Tolare and headed straight for the temple.

Jen felt no fear as they glided high above. The gem glowed, holding her on to his back. She felt safe, free and complete. The flight ended too soon for Jen as they reached the grounds of the temple buildings.

Iyon pranced to the center of the circular temple court covered by a metal dome and pounded the ground with his hoof. This sent the platform into a spinning motion and then it dropped straight down, casting them into the black abyss below the temple. There, they saw John on another floating platform already in the abyss with Hope. The first thing Jen noticed was that her father was finally wearing Tolarian clothes. He was kneeling on his knees with his eyes closed. Jared was also there, and Fox as well. They too were kneeling on their knees behind their friend. As soon as the platform that Jen was on was level with her fathers, she stepped onto it and came to be by her father's side, got on her knees and turned her head to look at him. Her eyes watered. All she wanted to do was embrace him. All those months of worry, doubt, and fear. And now here he was, next to her. She laid her head on his bony shoulder. He responded by wrapping his hand around her head. She in turn reached up and interlocked his hand with hers. They sat there like that for some time.

John sighed and opened his eyes. Tears smothered his face.

"That is everything, Hope. The whole account of my capture; nothing has been left out."

"I see. Let us not lose hope. Jen is here now and she will give her account of your rescue."

Over the next few minutes, Jen explained in as meticulous detail as she could her short-lived rescue experience. Jen gave her account of what she witnessed involving her father and what she had done to the Skeign in her anger. Then she went on to explain what she saw Iyon enduring when she returned with her father and saw his incredible fight with the Skeign. That caused a moment of silence in the room.

Hope then spoke up, "To Jen, I will say this. Now that a bond has formed between you and the Chest, there is much you will need to learn. You confessed you used your bond to exile a Skeign, and where you sent him, you do not know. Though this will hinder their advancement on us, it was accomplished with aggression and anger, for revenge was in your heart. You must understand that using the power of the Chest by your command through anger will begin a painful process of cutting the bond you have with it. It is a grave mistake you must not do again. For as you have been filled with something ancient, if that power dims; it will leave a void that you could very easily fill with something else, and that something else could be pure wickedness. This is a warning that you must adhere to. Now that you and the power of the Chest are joined, the responsibilities of this burden and the expectations on you will never again be the same."

As Hope continued explaining the Chest and her new responsibility, Jen's mind trailed to Micol, and what he must have felt like when responsibility was thrust upon him. He had no choice in his destiny; now, neither did she. A storm raged inside of Jen; one part of her longed for her old life back at home and yet another side of her loved the new one. Could she say she regretted knowing Iyon, or the many adventures they had already had together? Her heart answered for her. There was no way she would ever regret her experiences and adventures with Iyon.

"Jen? You are drifting." Her father eyed her.

"I'm sorry. This is all so much for me. Sometimes my mind trails elsewhere, but I'm doing the best I can."

Hope responded in kind, "We know that you are, and commend you for that. Now that your father is here, you will train under him. He will be your mentor and you will need to treat him as such. Are you both clear on this?"

"Yes," they said in unison.

"Time is short. Training will start now. Begin with touring the rest of the temple, and then the library. Cover as much history as you can today. And John, return to me at the end of the day for an account as well as instructions for tomorrow.

John nodded his head. "As you say."

The platform moved upward and soon the two were standing above ground in the temple dome. It wasn't until then that Jen noticed Iyon had stayed behind in the abyss, and Fox and the others took their leave.

"Dad, did you see what happened to Iyon?"

"Iyon has been weakened by the last attack. Hope takes him. What happens exactly I do not know. But he will be strengthened fully soon." John looked at his daughter, his eyes drifting down to the strap on Jen's shoulder. "Jen! Do you realize what you have there?" John was speechless; he really couldn't believe his eyes. He surmised the most logical explanation, "Adriana must have never gone back and retrieved it after that night. Well, I don't blame her." John put his head down in embarrassment. "I've waited months for this day to come, Jen. You deserve to know what happened that night. I'm sorry you had to wait so long to find out what happened between your mother and me. I was the one that decided to go into the woods that night. Come, follow me. Let me take you through the other temple buildings and we'll talk along the way."

Jen handed him the bag. That made him smile as he rhythmically threw it over his shoulder as he had always done throughout his life. Jen followed her dad into the inner temple corridors, a place she had not yet seen since she arrived in Tolare. John made sure there was no one around before he began to tell his story. When the halls were empty, he began to speak.

"Your mother tried to talk me out of it, but I was stubborn. I always had a love for adventure and seeking truth in the most mysterious of places. It got the better of me that night. 'Just for a little bit,' was what she said to me. Not too far into the forest, I swore I heard my name being called. I saw a light. I couldn't help but follow it. I know your mom yelled at me to stop, but I lost track of her voice. All I wanted to do was follow that light. I didn't realize how far I had run or where I had run to.

"That's when I saw the bark of a most peculiar tree split apart and Hope in all her transcendence appeared to me. We talked about incredible things before your mother arrived. She was outraged and frightened. She tried to pull me away but I refused and I was so frustrated with her. I dropped the bag, lost my balance and fell backwards. Once you get close to a portal like that, gravity from within it does the rest. I was pulled through and then it destabilized and closed." He hung his head down in shame. "I'm sorry, Jen. I should've been more careful."

"We're together now. So nothing else matters besides finding Mom." John tried to hide his emotions at the mention of his beloved. How would he tell his daughter where she could be?

"And since I'm with you here now, that means double the trouble for anyone who would dare oppose us," Jen chided confidently. This caused a smile to creep up across the sullen man's face. He looked at his bag Jen had brought for him.

"I never showed you what's in this," John said, changing the subject. "Let's go to the room of the scrolls. I want you to see." John led her through an arched doorway that opened to a temple courtyard full of delicate flowers, cared for by the groundskeepers. A set of large double doors engraved with carvings of all sorts of beautiful creatures opened and led to a room. The walls from ceiling to floor were lined with shelves containing thousands of scrolls, all of them organized by date. The ceiling was encrusted with layers of diamonds, igniting the room with iridescent light that came from within them. John and Jen sat at a table next to each other. John held the family heirloom in his hand and for a minute a thousand thoughts went through his mind. And then he opened the bag. To Jen's surprise, he pulled out a very old-fashioned quill pen along with a sealed small container of ink and four leather-bound journals that were closed with nothing more than very old-looking laced ribbon.

"Why four?"

John placed them side by side and pointed to them while answering. "This one is mine, my father's, my grandfather's, and then my great-grandfather's. Now I have read all the journals. I want to read this last page of my great-grandfather's journal to you. It's almost like he knew something would happen." John opened the journal and went to the last page. "Now listen to this, 'and today is the day I will present this leather bag to my beloved son to begin the family tradition of the legacy of the leather-bound journals so that our lives will never be forgotten, nor our grand adventures. And I have another grand story to add. But that will be written in my next journal. I hope someday to make sure that it will be safe in this bag of memories along with all the other journals. One never knows the turns of life, but we will always hope. Until then, happy birthday, my wonderful son.' And then he disappeared forever," John sadly concluded.

Jen stared at the journal as her father read it to her and memories of a leather-bound journal began to be recalled in her mind. She had seen it before…but where? And that's when it hit her. She stared at her father in complete child-like wonder and a grin formed from ear to ear.

"No, he didn't disappear, Dad. Your great-grandfather was a Key Holder."

Dumbfounded, he stammered, "Jen…how…why would you say that?"

She stood up and pointed to the journals, "Because of these! Next to the man that was in the cave where I found the Chest was a very, very old man. He wore overalls and had a carpenter's belt on." John slowly rose to his feet. "And by his side was a leather-bound journal."

"Are you telling me you saw my great-grandfather?"

"Yes! Dad, believe it! We have to get that journal. It must be filled with so many untold stories and secrets."

John's eyes lit like fire because so much bad had happened to him and his family. He gladly welcomed for something good to happen for a change. There was nothing more appetizing to him than solving a piece of their giant family mystery. It had plagued the family for years. And now, answers were finally coming together. Hope would have to be convinced—that wouldn't be easy; not after all that transpired over the past several days.

John hurriedly put the items back in his bag as he reasoned what should be done. The prospect of seeing the resting place of a lost loved one ignited him with energy and excitement. But he also knew that there was no time for this. Jen needed instruction, and that would have to come first. Yet, this was far too monumental to overlook. No, somehow, he would have to show Hope the importance of this trip; that it was not something to be dismissed.

. . . .

"So you're adamant about finding this man?" Hope asked questioningly.

"I believe it is most necessary. We need to learn as much about our enemy as he knows about us. My family has always kept detailed records in our journals. If we could get our hands on that journal, I know it would not be a waste of time. Imagine the secrets we could learn."

Hope spun within her orbit of radiant colors, quietly contemplating.

"This is interesting news, and quite a wonder as to how your great grandfather, William, ended up in Eshron all those years ago. I have no knowledge in any of our recorded history of this event. I will allow this mission to Eshron, but only because Eshron is now our ally and is currently at peace. No time is to be spent there among the people, John, no matter how much they beg you two to stay. Retrieve the journal and be back in a day's time.

"Normally, I would send you through myself, but then I never end up directly near the city, and Iyon would have to go and take you the rest of the way. Since the attack of Malum and the Tor, I will not be sending him with you. He is occupied at the moment."

"Jen, you can open a portal that takes you straight to the room in the palace that holds the golden globe that was the entrance to the world where you found the Chest. Don't waste time looking for anyone to explain why you are there. Hopefully, no one will be there so you can proceed to the next world. If someone is there, explain your mission, but do so quickly. Now go, and hurry back. We have very little time to mentor and train you for what is to come."

"We give our word," John promised. "Straight there and back. Besides, there are no forces that know of this journal. They will not anticipate our return to Eshron, so this will be under the enemy's radar."

Jen felt her entire body heat up from the inside out. An inconsolable force rushed through her. Feeling the unexplainable power of the river of light, Jen extended her hand and focused on their destination. A place she remembered well.

The sensations that came from the Ancient poured out of her. It overwhelmed every feeling, every member of her being as she submitted to the power. The vulnerability unnerved Jen and the vortex that had formed before them grew shaky.

Remember what I first told you when we met, Jennifer? That was your first and most important lesson from me.

Jen felt the oneness between them as the voice of the Ancient from the Chest soothed her soul.

I'm sorry. How could I forget?

Her breathing became slower as she recalled, the vortex stabilized, and she put her hand back down and looked toward Hope.

"That seemed a little harder than the last time," she confessed.

"There are strange and unusual forces at work during these days. Be on your guard. Above all, protect your minds. Now hurry," said Hope.

John and Jen turned and disappeared into the vortex.

Iyon, who was hidden within Hope and her transcendent glory, watched them vanish, and neighed in a low tone.

"They are unprotected. I do not feel right about it."

"You will draw more attention to them by going. They will be safe when they enter the next portal. If the vortex could've entered that world, it would've done so long ago, and so would our other enemies. I am not unaware of the bond you two have created, Iyon. If you feel cause for alarm, I will not hesitate to send you."

Iyon rested quietly within the rays of her being, and continued to replenish his body. He only hoped that if something did happen, he would make it there in time to help them.

Chapter 13
The Journal Mission

John and his daughter were standing in Celesta's old private library; the globe of the world was still present in its usual corner. To their advantage, no one was in the room to question them. In John's mind, the less time wasted, the better. Walking over to the globe together, they pulled the latch and opened the globe to reveal the portal inside. Jen did not move right away, but looked around instead. The library books and scrolls were replaced with weapons. There were shelves and shelves full of artillery, tasers, and even missile-like weapons.

"Seems like our army back at home has loaded them up," Jen commented.

"Jen," John called to her. "We need to leave here now." They entered into the next portal, ending up in the exact spot that Jen had, not too long ago.

The sun shone bright in the clear blue sky. The two trudged quickly across the field and into the forest. Jen led the way across the stream and they continued on for close to an hour before she reached the pool with the mysterious waterfall.

"Just wait until you see this, Dad."

John didn't respond. Instead he stood, gazing upon the waterfall as it fell over the cliff and into the pool. The sound of the splashing waves could be heard, yet the entire pool was completely still. Staring at the falling water was no different than staring into a mirror.

"Unfathomable," he finally said.

"Are you ready?" Her body trembled with excitement as reality set in that she was actually there with her father and could share this with him.

He smiled and waded into the water after her. As soon as they made it to the waterfall, Jen gave him a quick warning.

"Just keep walking. Don't stop and the waterfall will move around you. You won't even get wet." The passage through the waterfall happened the same as before. Just as Jen was about to touch the water that looked like a glass sheet, it separated around her and John, letting them through. It was like walking into a giant crystal ball. The light inside the room danced with crystals that covered the walls of the cave. The dance made the rainbow of colors fill the air. The two waded through the water, and then tenderly stepped up the diamond staircase. After reaching the top, they saw the resting place of John's great-grandfather.

Jen's delight faded as fast as it came when she saw where he had been lying. She went to his bedside to see the reality of this strange phenomenon. The diamonds had grown up all around him and over him, encasing him inside an impenetrable tomb. Jen looked through the fortified wall of solid crystal; his features had not changed since she last saw him. And there next to him, was the journal, encased in the solid crystal along with the Key Holder.

John knelt next to the tomb with a solemn look on his face. He resolutely said, "We pay our respects. His secrets I would say were meant to be buried with him."

"I wish I'd known him, or had a chance to tell him who I was when he was on his last breath," Jen exclaimed.

"It was impossible for you to know," he said. "And now to William, my great-grandfather; thank you for your simple ways and pureness of heart. And for the bag with the gift of a tradition you have started. Your sacrifice will not be forgotten."

As John finished, he stood up and placed his hand on top of the crystal tomb, and immediately, it sank through the shield like water. John's first reflex was to yank it back, but he couldn't. It was stuck fast.

Jen grabbed his free hand to steady him. "Whatever forces are here, it's letting you do this. Go ahead, Dad. Get the journal."

John grimaced at first, not liking the fact that his arm was trapped in his great-grandfather's tomb. Since he couldn't pull it out, he reached down for the journal and grasped it firmly. The force freed him and John pulled his arm out freely. With the book in hand, he silently walked over to the diamond steps and sat down. Jen joined him and together they opened the book.

Entry 1

I cannot in fathomable words describe what has transpired over the course of these last few days. What I can tell you is that something took me from my family and home. What this something is, I do not know. How it is alive and talks to me, I do not know. But unless I cooperate with it, it will never again let me see my loved ones or home ever again. My heart aches this night, but for now I will play its friend, and journey through these caves to see if I can find my way home. I am sorry I am not with you, my lovely Janine and dear child, John. Keep strong. I will return to you as soon as I can. This is William John Hanning, and I am lost and in need of help. Until my next entry, fare thee well.

By the end of the read, John's face was streaked with tears. The mystery of what had happened to William was finally revealed. Years of bearing the yoke of the unknown lifted off his shoulders as at last, John knew he would find out everything that happened to William.

Jen rested her head on her father's shoulder and the two sat there as a strange and familiar presence filled their minds.

John....Jen....

How strange, I feel like I've just heard my mother's voice, thought Jen.

No!!!

The two were in a trance, unable to move until John shook it off, jumped to his feet and anxiously grabbed Jen's shoulder to pull her out of it.

"Jen!" She looked up at him.

"That was so strange, Dad. I think I heard Mom's voice just now."

"We're in trouble. We need to leave now," was all John could say.

As she jumped up to leave, she sent a thought to Iyon. *Iyon, something is wrong. Can you hear me? Find us.*

John held the book above the water and the two cautiously made their way out through the waterfall. As soon as they reached the other side, John paused and listened to nature. The sounds of the singing birds filled the air, making them relax again.

"Everything looks okay to me, Dad. Let's get home as fast as we can," stated Jen.

"Agreed."

The two were near the edge of the waters and began to climb out. A monstrous force struck the water. John held the book to his chest, fearing what was behind them. They did not have a chance to look back. A tentacle wrapped around each of them, picked them up and threw them onto the dry ground. John thrust the book into the inner pocket of his cloak as the tentacles wrapped around his chest and legs, squeezing the life out of him. A dozen Skeign pounced from behind the falls and in seconds, both of them were held captive.

John couldn't help but cry out in pain as the memories of what the Skeign would do to them flooded his mind. Hearing the screams of his daughter broke John's heart. A horrific roar vibrated their ears. Prisoners now, they were turned toward the pool. It was the Skeign leader of that patrol. The leader Skeign's black oily fur reeked of death and its claws dragged and pulled the earth up with it as it came out of the water, growling in delight as drool dripped from its razor sharp fangs.

"Enough of your screaming! Master will be pleased you have been found. Come, beasts! To the exit with our prisoners!"

The two were picked up; the ground began to rumble as another more fearsome growl came from the waterfall. As the creatures turned to flee with their prey, its fearless leader near the water's edge was suddenly picked up by strands of water that came directly from the waterfall. What once was a sheet of water that looked like a mirror suddenly changed. The water separated into hundreds of slashing whips. The diamonds from within became jagged razor-sharp teeth as a roar came from the black abyss that now filled the mouth of this mysterious cave. The rocks moved rhythmically together and formed the head of an animal. The strands of water were as strong as metal and wrapped around the Skeign leader that was in the pool. It picked that creature up and hurled it into its mouth. The Skeign leader howled bitterly and disappeared.

The Skeign that were holding John and Jen tried fleeing from the falls to escape, but the faux animal head formed by the strands of water were too fast for them. In seconds it attacked, whipping and devouring them all. The tentacles holding John and Jen were sliced through, and they fell safely to the ground. John turned over and jumped to his feet. He grabbed his daughter's arm and helped her up, and they started to run for the woods. The sound of a thousand more Skeign came from behind the waterfall. Dread filled John, as he knew that there was no way they would make it to the portal entrance.

The monstrous waterfall roared and extended two strands of water; gathered them both and flung them high into the sky toward the direction of the portal entrance. They were both screaming frantically, powerless as to what their fate would be now. Was the water monster helping them, or causing them harm? A friend or a foe? John grabbed for Jen's arm and yelled as loud as he could.

"Jen! You have to make a vortex beneath us as we fall."

Just as John finished saying this, they began to lose altitude, falling back toward the earth. As John held onto one hand, Jen pointed her other down as best she could, but nothing happened. The two were rapidly approaching the ground.

Figuring that they would die, he brought her closer to him. They shut their eyes while holding one another, not wanting to know when the end would come.

And that's when he came. Appearing like a flash of light in the sky, Iyon had found them. He rescued them, swooping underneath them as they tumbled to the ground, and the two safely sat on his back while still embracing one another.

Gasping for breath, Jen concentrated on slowing her racing heartbeat. "How? What?"

Iyon flipped his neck around to give her a quick gaze. "I heard your call and Hope sent me immediately to the silver shores of Eshron where you and I first came to that world."

As soon as he felt Jen in trouble, Hope sent Iyon to the silvery shores of Eshron where he flew over the cliffs and smashed through the walls of the castle until he reached the golden globe. It was no small disturbance, and the damage he caused was almost catastrophic to the structure. Iyon pounded through the portal within the globe and took to the air. That's when he saw them falling right out of the sky.

"Thank you," she murmured, leaning close to his ear. "You were there when I needed you. When we needed you."

"My pleasure," he replied and he swooped in the air and headed back to the portal as John bear hugged his daughter, with the sound of the roaring Skeign not far behind.

Iyon pounded into the room. The king with a company of soldiers were guarding the globe, their weapons in hand; aiming at the portal.

Iyon commanded, "Get back! I'm destroying the portal!"

In a matter of seconds, John and Jen slipped off Iyon's back and ran for the door. The company of soldiers grabbed their king and thrust him toward the door in order to protect their king from the blast. The untold power of the gem ignited like an explosion. Iyon's body glowed from the immense power within. His eyes flared all the colors that radiated from Hope herself. Just a couple seconds before a monstrous Skeign army could come through the portal, Iyon released a blast from within his eyes that combined with the power that came from the gem. It hit the globe and the ancient portal; bursting it into a million fragments. The weapons blew off the shelves as a tornado of air formed in the room, then faded into nothing, leaving the room utterly destroyed.

Iyon looked back for the king and his friends and found them safe, buried under the guards who threw themselves over them, protecting them just outside the library doors.

"My sincere apologies, King Rozor. We cannot stay this time and clean up the mess I made. Malam and Tor are hunting me. I assure you we will send immediate aid until everything is fixed."

The king was still distraught but took in everything Iyon had said. Knowing that the Warrior would keep his word, he nodded. "We will anticipate the aid. If Malum is after you, then leave quickly, my friend."

Iyon turned to Jen, "Form a vortex now. I do not want to cause more trouble for these people."

Jen held up her hand and instantly the river within her rushed out through her hand. The vortex formed and the three of them disappeared quickly through it. Though Jen said nothing, her confusion of why she could not form a portal and save them when they were falling to their death terribly frustrated her. What happened in that world and how the Skeign came to be in it was a horrifying reality of how the scales were quickly turning not for the better.

Chapter 14
The Pact with the Beast

"We missed another opportunity! We should've kept an eye on Eshron!" Malum growled, and turned away from the vortex in disgust.

"Hope is keeping Iyon in Tolare now to protect him from us. Tracking him whenever and wherever he may show up is proving to be a tedious and cumbersome task," the vortex retorted. "But there is another way," said Tor.

"Yes," Malum interjected, as if both were thinking the same evil. "There is another way. We need to get to Eshron now. Since Hope is trying to protect her asset, let's draw him out ourselves."

"Not yet," whispered Tor. "First, there's another world we need to visit, and a great Beast."

Malum grunted disapprovingly, but knew what it was talking about it, "So be it then," and he disappeared into the vortex.

············

It was upon the steps of Tran, where Dolorous resided within the thick black clouds, filled with thunder and lightning, that Malum appeared with Tor.

All the Skeign there growled, roared and snarled at the foolish bravery of these hated enemies, but dared not to move without orders from Dolorous.

Dolorous, out of pure fury, emerged out of the clouds in the physical form of a black dragon, and stood before them, making them look like nothing more than grasshoppers compared to his great size. There was a contentious look of pleasure in his eyes. His dinner was delivered right to him. And since this pathetic creature had the audacity of showing up on his temple steps it could only mean death, at least for the black horse. But when his eyes beheld Tor, the swirling anomaly that was behind the horse; he slightly bowed his head and trembled in sensational delight.

"You," Dolorous snarled, looking at the Warrior Horse blackened from evil, "Are a perverse creature that should not exist! Come closer to me, so I can devour you and put an end to your vile existence."

"Hold your tongue, dragon," Malum bravely spoke. "I am the essence of pure evil, no different than you! How can you say that I am vile? Should we quarrel when our enemies are the same? Do we not both hate the same beings, Hope and Iyon, and all the treachery they stand for?"

The very sound of the names of his hated enemies caused an uncontrollable rage to rise in Dolorous. Fire and smoke bellowed from his mouth as he repeated their names.

Malum continued, "Why not work together? Just how many in your army has Iyon destroyed? Is he not a thorn to your Master's side?"

Dolorous growled, "Your stupid questions will get you devoured, horse. Get to your point."

"I want your Master to command the army to stay out of my way as I go after Iyon. If they would have stayed out of my way on Shadow Earth, he would've already been mine. Instead, the army was sent out and thwarted my plans. Upon the thousands that attacked, none could kill him. Your army disgraces your Master greatly. This is my pact with you. I will deliver the girl to the lair of your Master. All I ask is that Iyon's destruction be left to me, and leave us alone in any world that we need to travel. I have plans to make him suffer before he is destroyed. Are we agreed?"

Fire and smoke fumed from his nostrils as Dolorous considered Malum's proposition, then came to his decision.

"I will speak with the Master and ask that he order his servants to stand down if you are seen in any of the worlds. They will not advance on you or the penalty will be death. When the girl is captured, take her to the Master's throne, and bring her father as well if he is not already captured by then. If you fail, then you will die next time we meet."

"Very well," Malum snorted, then turned and exited through the vortex. Tor did not vanish immediately but lingered afterwards. It stared at the black dragon. If it had eyes, they would be filled with mockery and fearlessness toward this formidable enemy in front of it. It had been in prison so long, and now, to be finally free made it shamelessly bold.

Dolorous growled in disgust, but then consented with a question. "Why do you continue to work with such a lowly creature, One that is more powerful than I? I speak for my Master, Aged One; for I know he desires you. Only together, will he rule over True Earth, and all of its other dimensions. What holds you back from this great destiny? Still questioning your fate?"

The swirl within the vortex spun silently around. "I am finally free to do what I want. Tell your Master I am free to do as I please, for he is not my Master," and then Tor diminished from sight.

"Only for a short time, are you free. You will be called upon by the Master. When the reign of Darkness begins; you, Aged One, will become his."

Laughing contemptuously, the black dragon turned and stomped back into the thunderous cloud that filled the temple's center. The Skeign all around roared in agreement, and bowed their beastly heads low to the ground until the temple clouds enveloped Dolorous, and he could be seen no more.

Meanwhile, the vortex took Malum back to the Abyss World, where the wind always blew, the storms always raged and evil lurked. This became Malum's home long ago. It both destroyed him and rebuilt him.

"Do you wish to attack Eshron now?" Tor asked Malum.

"No, not just yet. Keep an eye on them every so often. If you see them packing and filling up wagons, then we'll have to begin operations against them, but if not, then they will be there for the picking when we are ready. First, we need to gather supplies from the other worlds. Now that we are free to roam without being attacked, it should not be so cumbersome. I will take great pleasure in it for a short while. Iyon will show his face eventually. We need to prepare for the next time he leaves Tolare. That is all that matters. And when Iyon has been dealt with, we will ransack Eshron, take its people as prisoners and level the city. It will be a sign to all others the cost if you are associated with Iyon or even Tolare. When that time comes, there is nothing the peasants will be able to do to stop us, but I will take pleasure in them trying. There is much we need to build here as the peasants will need to be held as prisoners. Mother will be so pleased with such a great gift. So let's go, there is much work to do and I look forward to what is to come."

Tor, the vortex anomaly, followed Malum to the jagged mountain system and began to prepare the wicked plan of sadistic revenge.

....

Adriana awoke from her deep trance. Her plush chair she had been lying in was damp from her sweat. With her eyes still closed, she reached for a towel that was lying on a circular glass table next to the meditation chair. She wiped her face and sat up.

"Feeling okay, Adriana?"

"Oh!" Adriana jumped in her seat, her heart skipping a beat. She saw the outline of a familiar figure standing off in a darkened corner. Her body relaxed; it was Liel, her mentor. Her mind drifted back to the time she had first met him in the woods when she was so lost and frail. Her path was full of darkness and he shown light on it, renewing her hope that one day, she would be with John again.

"Uh, yeah. Don't know if I'm getting the hang of this though. I don't see how meditating and constantly talking to them in my mind is going to do anything. I've been at this for days; weeks, if you include the times I've tried from the woods before I even came here."

Liel chuckled under his breath and moved out of the dim corner. She couldn't help but notice that he always wore clothes similar in color, over and over. It was always jeans, a white collared shirt with black casual shoes to go with it. Everything was always crisp and brand new looking. His smile seemed gentle and warm.

"Far more than you could ever imagine, my dear. We were able to trace their location through the connection you established and almost retrieved them not too long ago. We will find them. Just be patient, keep doing what you're doing."

Adriana's spirit lifted when he said this. She pulled herself out of the chair with what strength she had left and went over to him. "Almost retrieved him! You mean….it worked? You found them?" The excitement repulsed Liel, but at least this woman was happy to serve him. He smiled to make her think that he was proud of her efforts, when he really was smiling at being that much closer to his end game. And when he had achieved that, he would delightfully take her soul as soon as he was done with her.

"Yes, Adriana, you did it. You should be proud of yourself."

"Well….that's great. But what happened? Why wasn't it fully successful?"

Liel looked away as he spoke to her, as pestering questions annoyed him to no end. However, he knew this body action would build emotion and suspense, so he played this out to utter perfection. Liel gazed down at the floor with a defeated and helpless look, his hands buried in his pockets. "What usually happens," looking back up at her with sadness in his eyes. "Some force of nature prevented our retrieval posse from acquiring them. The whole company of them was killed in the process, no doubt the doing of Iyon and those rebels!"

"I'm sorry," said Adriana, feeling guilty in some way for the ones that were killed because of her own family. "I'll rest up and try again. I'll keep doing whatever I did that worked. I promise that I will try even harder next time."

Liel got exactly what he wanted from her, a stronger commitment to enslave herself even deeper than before.

He touched her cheek with his hand, "I know you will. And I know you're trying. But it is imperative we find them next time before any more damage is done by them or more lives taken. So much depends on it. I know I can count on you. I feel the next time you come back you should just concentrate on your daughter. John is much too strong for us right now. But your daughter may not be. Think only of her." He ended with an allusive smile on his face.

"For now, go to your new room you can now call your home; clean up and eat. When you're ready, then come back and we'll try again."

"New room?" Adriana said in confusion.

"Yes. For your hard labor, you have been awarded an upgrade to a more luxurious and spacious penthouse living space. It's just a small token from me to show my…appreciation for what you do."

Adriana couldn't help but to smile at his kind words to her. "Well I can't wait to see it," she said graciously.

"There is an attendant outside the door waiting for you. He will take you there. I will see you later."

"Fine. Well, good-day then," she nodded and left the room; the door slowly closed on its own behind her.

Once the door sealed shut and automatically locked, Liel looked toward the wall on the opposite side of the room where her meditation chair was placed. Liel waved his hand from right to left. The content of the wall changed into a gel substance making it possible to walk through. Liel beckoned with his hand for his servant to come to him. A small red dragon came through the wall. With fear and trembling, she came and bowed before the Master. This dragon's body was almost totally deformed now and covered with hideous scars from endless days of torture that befell her from the shameful failures of the past. She was once a beautiful dragon, but no longer. One more mistake would mean eternal condemnation. The time of decision had come for her. Had she done enough to please her Master and turn his wrath from her? The beaten dragon lowered her head down to his feet and there she remained until he would decide.

"Much better, Escapist. I cannot say well done since we do not have them here, however, that is something I will not blame you for. Meld with Adriana's mind again when she comes back and continue to make your presence in her a secret. When she is in a state of vulnerability, manipulate her thoughts to draw Jen away from Tolare. Succeed in this and I may yet restore your honor from the cursed ignorance you displayed of letting Jen escape from you in the first place. Fail me and your former punishment will be nothing in comparison to what I will do to you."

Trembling in absolute fear, she nodded while still bowing, and then squeamishly exited back through the wall; thankful for the extended grace she had been given.

Liel stood motionless after Escapist had left and began to calculate his next moves when a familiar but much unexpected presence entered his domain. He could sense it was one of his most respected Commanders who had come seeking counsel with him, and he did so without permission. Liel's brow cringed in great disappointment.

How could he leave his post!?!

. . . .

The Master's immense throne room could hold a thousand dragons. It was dismal and barren, and the walls stretched upward for what seemed like a mile. There were no gems or statues to fill it. There were but a few lanterns fashioned out of iron casting off a grayish light. Where a throne chair would normally be found, there was nothing more than a large platform, raised several feet above the floor. Only by invitation of the king could one enter this room. Yet standing tall and proud in front of the large stone platform was Dolorous.

He was a monstrous black dragon, his ebony scales still glistened even in the bleakest of light. There was not one slash mark inflicted from any punishment on this beast. His flawless service and countless victories placed him high above any other dragon. That was why he was given legions of Skeign to command and why he was chosen for the mission in Tranquil Earth with the taking of Tran. But never did Dolorous suspect such complication subduing the enemy. He did not consider the being in that world to have the capability of exiling herself while at the same time, finding a way to be a thorn that constantly pierced his pride.

He certainly had not calculated the damage that one lone Warrior

Horse could do as well. Now they had built an army somewhere under his nose, ending his flawless record and ultimately humiliating him. Dolorous wanted nothing more than to rid himself of that wretched horse, and redeem his honor. He also knew that coming uninvited to see the Master was grounds for death on a good day, but thought the news he had would save him from that fate. And so he stood in front of his Master with great confidence.

From behind the platform, Liel emerged, purposefully in human form. He walked in and stood in the center of the platform, glaring at Dolorous with deep contempt in his eyes.

Seeing the Master in such a form, Dolorous knew that he was not pleased with his actions, and so would not give him the pleasure or respect of letting him see himself in his true nature.

As Liel spoke, the words coming from his mouth sounded like a ravenous lion ready to kill. "Dolorous, I gave you a highly desired job. It was an honor, but it came with one command, and you broke it. So how torturous and publically humiliating should the death of a great Commander be?"

Dolorous bowed his head. "I am a faithful servant to my Master. I would not have left without good reason."

"You left your post!" The power in Liel's voice shook the walls of the hall and echoed throughout his entire underground kingdom, except for the forbidden sector, where he kept the humans. Now all would know that one of their own would surely die this day.

Dolorous did not move a muscle as he heard the doors at the back of the throne room open. Two black monstrous beasts stood in the doorway, holding great chains in their hands. They were the dungeon masters and stood quietly, awaiting their orders.

Lowering his voice, Liel spoke again. "You never leave your post."

"Do what you must with me, but the message I bring is not one I would ever give the honor to another to deliver. My message today triggers the dawn of your great reign of True Earth. The start of an ancient prophecy you have long awaited to be fulfilled."

Liel stared at the beasts in the back. In shock, they slowly backed away from the doors, hoping the Master would change his mind. Never before had the Keepers of the dungeons left without dragging the condemned with them; it was an utter disappointment. They lowered their heads in disgust as Dolorous would have been their finest prize. The doors shut behind the black monsters, leaving Dolorous alone in the room with Liel.

"Go on, Dolorous. I will let you finish this message."

"The Aged One, who likes to be called Tor, has been freed from its prison that the Ancient put it in so long ago. It came to me with the rogue Warrior Horse. They are freelancing about all our realms as we speak. They wish, Great Master, to make a pact with us, and be left alone so they can bring Iyon to an end. But you see, my Master, Tor has been freed. This means that soon, it will be yours and your reign will begin."

"Dolorous," the Master said quite pleasantly, "this is good news. Now, the scales are tipped in my favor. Hope and all the realms she protects will not stand against me now. How interesting," Liel let out a devious laugh, "that the Aged One…I mean Tor, would want to run about like a foolish child with a perverted Warrior Horse that should not even exist. I want that black beast for myself. Its very presence is an abomination to evil. That thing must be destroyed by me. Let them be for now. We will honor this so-called pact. Then, when it's time, I will call the Aged One back to me. How ironic to think it is free to choose its destiny when it rightfully belongs to me! If it wants a fight, so be it," exclaimed Liel.

Dolorous snarled. "The Warrior's name is Malum."

Liel stood for a moment, letting his mind flash through history, looking for one that was ever called Malum, but none came to mind. What proved more a mystery than that was how the Warrior, if giving his soul over to evil, had not transformed into a Skeign, which is the outcome of all Warriors who are succumbed by the power of the darkness. The desire to consume this foul beast festered inside of him. But for now, Malum would prove to be a useful benefit for Liel and the plans he had.

"Let them cause pain to our enemies where we cannot. If his plan causes suffering, then it can do us no harm; I'll give the order. If they are seen anywhere in the realms, for now, they will not be harmed. It was both wise and foolish of you to come yourself. I thought this day I would be condemning one of my best. You, Dolorous, are free to return to Tran. I believe soon, it will be under your complete control."

Dolorous bowed his head, "Yes, Master."

He circled back around and withdrew from the throne room.

The Master was alone again. He stared at his flesh-covered hands. The sight of him portraying such a pathetic existence enthralled his hatred even more for those insolent creatures whose presence he bore the resemblance of. His eyes glowed like burning sapphire and the flesh under his jeans and shirt blazed and smoldered. The real monster inside was craving to break out.

The ashen colored walls depicted a pallid red that soon permeated the entire hall. Though he'd captured so many of these humans, and thrived off their sorrows, pain and bondage, it was never enough. He wanted more. His eyes fixed on the biggest prize, the hub of all the worlds, True Earth. To dominate that and feed off those that resided there was his end game plan. Despite all his legions of slaves and his army of dragons, he could never before defeat True Earth. Liel knew his plan would work. He would have to go about this very sagaciously, sly and cunning. Tor, as it is called for now, will be needed in order for that world to tear itself apart.

The Master subdued himself. The crimson glow faded and, with a new set of clothes covering his body, he left his hall. There was work to be done.

Chapter 15
The Reading of the Journal

After almost a week of searching, Jen finally had found it!

Clever Dad, hiding the journal in an empty water jug in the middle of Dahlia's garden, should've known. Jen stashed it inside her cloak and crept back into Dahlia's home. She was back asleep before anyone knew she had snuck out.

In the morning, Jen wasted no time eating her breakfast. She told her father to hurry up so they could get to the temple for more studying of the scrolls. She could see it pleased John to see her so anxious to learn today, unfortunately, that wasn't Jen's real reason for wanting to get there.

The two made their way into the building just west of the temple and found their way to the library of scrolls, where they spent every day since the moment they got back from Eshron. This study was an oval-shaped room with shelves lining the walls. The shelves held books and scrolls. It was built up, stone by stone, by the refugees in the village. The scrolls contained all of Tranquil Earth's history, as well as the history of many other worlds. For the past several days, Jen was made to learn the names and locations of the many worlds of Earth. At times, the information her father pounded into her head pushed her to the limit. She was required to study pictures of dozens and dozens of locations upon the other worlds of Earth. They were like a mystery to Jen. The memorization came with incredible ease throughout the training; however Jen wondered why she was studying these locations.

When Jen was busy reading over the scrolls, John was called away, leaving her alone in the library. When John had left, she whipped out the journal and opened it up. She hated having to hide it from her father. But John was the type of man who always had to follow steps. For him, studying the scrolls was first and the journal second. Well that didn't work for Jen and what she wanted to do. She looked down in great anticipation and began to read.

Entry 2

I made the mistake of putting my journal away for a number of days as I have been in shock from all that has happened. So to catch up, I will simply say this: I traversed out of the maze of caves into a city of magic and wonders. The people there brought me to their queen, Miriam, and she welcomed me with open arms. She was so kind to me during my time of need, and I wanted to repay her. I asked for wood and tools and crafted a marvelous treasure chest in the castle's workshop. Little did I know that by making that chest, it would lead to a fateful life for me. I know what happened to me by human standards seemed unfair, but now I see plainly what I am meant to do. I am a Key Holder with no Key, so now I will spend my life choosing to protect the amazing object of untold power and wonder that sits here before me. This is William John Hanning, and my family may never know what became of me, yet I feel that by the oddest means possible, I am protecting them to the greatest degree....

Oncoming footsteps headed down the hall. Her father's steps made it sound as if he was forever in a rush. She knew full well what that meant, a mind too full of thoughts. It always made John walk faster when he was deep in thought. Jen closed the journal and stuffed it inside of the pocket of her tunic, upset that she had to stop. She buried her head in the scrolls, reading away as he entered the room.

"Jen?" called John as he headed to another table across the study room "Have you finished reading that scroll yet? I wanted you to have read that in order to understand the culture and times this world had before the fall."

"Uhhh, yeah, Dad, I have," was all she could come up with.

John could tell when she was distracted. She would always grab the ends of her hair on the back of her head and twirl it around. It was a habit and a dead giveaway.

"What's distracting you?"

"I'm not distracted," she protested.

"Did you forget I'm your father? I know when you're distracted and when you're lying. So out with it."

How can I tell my dad the truth without giving myself away? And then the idea hit her.

"I want to read the journal."

John studied her body motion and facial expressions and could clearly tell that she was telling the truth.

"I know you're a little upset I hid the journal."

"A little?" she interjected with sass.

In a sterner tone, he said, "I won't bother bringing it out for you to read until you get through a few of the scrolls here. I also want to see a change of attitude."

"I don't have an attitude, Dad."

He pointed to her and quickly responded, "You see, there it is. Right there; that snap in your voice."

"Well, that's not attitude. I'm just frustrated and can't ever talk to you about it because you take everything as an attitude problem."

John stared at his indignant daughter in disbelief. He had no clue where this came from. Jen realized she had gone too far and tried to make a quick recovery.

"Look, Dad, I'm sorry. It's just that…you know how I love a good mystery. That journal is like a mystery waiting to be solved and I want to solve it. How do you think I did so well in school all the time?"

Please work, oh please, please work!

John let out a sigh, "Well, okay. I understand. How about this, tomorrow night you and I can sit down and read it together for a bit before bed. Sound good?"

Yes!

"That sounds great! Thanks. I'll get back to work now," Jen said with a huge smile on her face.

Their conversation was interrupted by a loud knock at the door, and then it abruptly opened. One of the sentinels from the temple came in.

"Greetings; I'm sorry to interrupt you with your studies. Hope wishes to speak with you right away."

"Am I going?" asked Jen.

"It's for military purposes. I was told to only bring John," said the sentinel.

"Yes, of course," John replied right away, then turned to Jen, "Continue reading the scroll until you are done with that one. When I get back, I'll quiz you because I know everything in that."

John hurriedly left to follow the guard out. For a little while, Jen continued to read the scroll her father had given her. But slowly the temptation to read the journal took over her. In great trepidation, she inched the journal out of her tunic pocket. She opened it and skimmed through a few entries that dealt with his travels through the lands she herself traversed when she was bound by the vine. They seemed like average entries. As she continued skimming, one entry caught her attention.

Entry 7

I find myself in front of this peculiar Chest, wondering how many weeks it has been since I last wrote in this journal? I've lost track of the days, of time in general, but at least I understand now why this box must be kept safe. Having time with it even as it remains unopened has let me feel what must be inside. I am waiting for the one that actually has the key. Lately, I have been thinking of the one who brought me to Eshron. I think back to the day I went into the woods back in my home world where I lived with my loving wife. There before me as I strolled along came spinning clouds, something like a horizontal whirlwind. It swept me up and transported me to Eshron and there I met the Queen. But before I ventured up and out into that unknown world, I had a conversation with the spinning clouds. It said that I was the first human it was ever able to take. Until then, all of its powers were trapped. The stalactites and stalagmites around this vile thing breathed a great delight when it mentioned that they formed its prison and held it there. The spinning clouds promised many great and wonderful things to me if I would share my soul with it. I promised that thing that I would never leave it alone. But some things are better off left imprisoned. Some things are better off forgotten. So the day came for me to leave through the portal found inside the globe in Queen Miriam's study. I wanted to warn her of its presence, but I didn't. I wanted no one to know of its existence, though I was the one who promised to help it. Its abilities brought fear to my innermost being. Now, I am an honest man and I do not break my promises, yet I felt I must this time. So I am confessing here in my journal for the ill I have bestowed on another. May those spinning clouds never be found, is all I can hope for.

Jen closed the journal and breathed a long sigh as the insight had a profound impact on everything she knew. The fact that it was her family member somehow brought here by the vortex that now sought to capture her and Iyon all made sense. It had been abandoned and lied to, so now it was wild, free and very dangerous. Did it know who she was? Surely if it did, it would have dealt with her earlier. Perhaps that secret was still safe, for now. As she looked at the journal, the question remained, should she dare continue?

"Well, can't stop now," she whispered under her breath, eager to learn more secrets.

Entry 8

I have waited a year before writing again. My life may go on for a very long time, and my pages are limited. So I had chosen not to write again until a home has been found for the Chest and me. I have finally found an amazing home for us. It is filled with sparkling wonders and secret rooms, opened up for me to explore. These rooms were furnished for me by the magic in this great place. This past year I have spent many days in those rooms, building, crafting, and waiting. How much longer, Key Holder, until you come and relieve me of my charge? Who will you be?

Jen winced as she realized the words were directly pertaining to her.

Yes, today is another calm day; nothing out of sorts took place. Until my next journal entry – William John Hanning

The last part of the journal entry did not make sense to Jen as the remainder of the page was blank. Yet every other page was completely filled. *I wonder.......* She ran the journal over to a lighted torch and held it up. The rest of the words were revealed by the torches' light. With this revealed message, Jen ran back to her table and sat down to read it.

After so many years of guarding this Chest I feel I know you, the one that is to come after me. So the rest of this entry is for you and you alone. I have not spoken of everything concerning the spinning vortex. I know its true name. It declared to me that its name was Lawless, and that it desired to spread its goodwill to others. So be leery of this Lawless entity. The day that the cursed thing is released will surely be the start of terrible times. And then the end will come. All endings allow for a new beginning. But times will get very dark indeed.

Take heart, my dear Jennifer Hanning, daughter of my son's son, for I know now that you are the Key Holder and are the one who will read these words. There will undoubtedly come a time when all hope seems lost. But do not give in to that. Become one with what is in the Chest and I'm telling you the truth, that order will be restored. –William John Hanning

Jen slammed the journal shut and shoved it across the table. Trapped in fear, she sat and trembled, unable to find strength to get up and move.

Then she felt a familiar warmth as if her mother was right there, wrapping her arms around her. Her fears dissipated for a brief moment, but then the feeling was gone as quick as it came.

What is happening to me?

Jen needed to talk to somebody that could understand her. *Micol!*

Remembering that he had been sent to the Temple to remain there, Jen brushed aside the thoughts of Iyon's orders to not pursue him right now and left the scroll room to search for him. Before heading down the hallway, Jen heard her father's footsteps swiftly approaching. Then she recalled that she left the journal on the table. Impulsively, she ran back into the room and hid the journal back in her tunic pocket. Jen was sitting back in her chair poring over the scrolls when he opened the door.

She looked up candidly at him, "Oh hi, Dad, back so soon?" Her face was stricken pale. John noticed that look and eyed his daughter with great disappointment as he walked right over to her.

John held out his hand. "I know you have it. Hand it over."

"What?"

"Now, Jen. Dahlia just came to the temple. She let me know."

Reluctantly, Jen pulled the journal out and handed it over to her father.

"Don't you want to find Mom?" she retaliated in anger. "How is poring over these scrolls going to help us with that? We've barely left this room since we've been back. I just really need a break."

John glared at his daughter. Her growing resistance was becoming a concern to him, not to mention trying to put him on a guilt trip about his wife.

"Tell me, the power contained in the Chest; where did it come from? What stories are foretold about it and what things are yet to come? Why does it link to you, what is the significance of a Key Holder, and how do you become one in order for it to truly work through you? Can you answer those questions yet? I've given you the information contained in the scrolls to read to help you understand better before you stand before the Chest again. And I have not forgotten about your mother. You know this, Jen."

What am I doing? Jen's mind cleared and she felt horrible for posing such a question to him after he had just faced incredible odds over the past several months. "I'm sorry, Dad. I don't know what got into me. I felt so impatient and compulsive. I didn't mean to say it. Perhaps I am just tired."

"We need to take a break, Jen. Let's go for a walk and get some fresh air."

Oh no, thought Jen. That meant that John had bad news.

"Sure, why not?" she consented.

Jen timorously got up and followed her father out into the woods behind the temple.

Chapter 16
The Walk in the Woods

The balmy breeze cascaded down the slopes, blew over the treetops and buffeted the brush below the forest canopy.

John and Jen walked side by side; the serene silence meant unwelcome news, Jen could feel it.

"So…is this about Mom?" Jen blurted out, no longer able to hold it in.

"It has to do with her, yes," he replied, his sorrow and frustration evident.

"Hope…has been making some connections, between the troubles I had in Shadow Earth, and the Skeign appearing in that hidden world where they had no business being."

"What are you trying to say?" she interrupted, dreading what was to come next.

"There was a reason they were able to find me, a reason they knew exactly where to find us by the falls."

"Dad, stop! I hope you're not trying to say what I think you're saying!"

"Be honest with me; Jen, how often has your mother been on your mind?"

Jen began shaking her head in denial; her heart pounded wildly in her chest along with a pain that she felt could kill her. "Don't say it. Don't tell me."

"Adriana is aiding the enemy."

Jen exploded. Not with tears but with anger. "Well, you're wrong! If she is there, then she is being forced and tortured as you were. We have to get her back! We have to go….leave right now!"

"We can't. There's more to this."

"Yes, we can! Let's just go; you and me," she demanded.

"Hope has given an order. We are not to leave Tolare for any reason right now."

"That's crazy! I was promised that she would be saved!" Jen pounded his chest, "I can't believe you're just going to sit back and do nothing, not even for my mother…your wife!"

Jen turned and stormed away, but yelled back to him as she left. "Just leave me alone! You've all lost your minds."

"Well that didn't go over so well at all," John said out loud to himself. He didn't even have a chance to say why they couldn't leave Tolare.

The sound of galloping hooves could be heard coming from the temple. Iyon came up next to John and stopped.

"Hello, John. The messenger has been sent to King Rozor and has told him what we have decided on for Eshron. Hope has ordered Jared to mobilize the troops to be sent there, and has put Taq in charge of the units deploying. Jared is not to go since Malum is in search of him. We have at most three weeks to fix what is going on with Jen and have her fully trained and ready for what needs to be done."

"I'd like to think that Eshron wouldn't get an attack from Malum and Tor, but I know that's just whimsical thinking. I wish I could help them," said John.

"If I can get through to Jen, you will be of help in the way we need you to be. Let's hope the planned diversions will work long enough for the troops to get settled and the villagers to evacuate. But enough of that; how is she?"

"I didn't get very far with her. She stomped off before I could tell her everything. Something very bad is happening. I felt an oppression in my mind that I've been contending with since I was trapped in Shadow Earth. I have been strong against it, and now it's gone. I fear the worst, Iyon. I believe the attacks are directed solely at Jen now."

"I know," Iyon said solemnly. "I can sense her anger building. I will go and try to talk with her. She needs to fight who is attacking her. This was an unexpected strategic attack and will hinder any chance she has of progressing."

John dug his hands into his pockets, knowing the truth and gravity of the situation.

"Hope wants to see you again. You are also a Key Holder. Open the Chest, and prepare yourself."

John hated the fact that Jen was falling for the deception and he was helpless at the moment to save his daughter. She would have to choose to fight this on her own.

"Alright," John said, "But please find me once you've talked with her. I will go and do what I must."

"Certainly. I will be in touch with you soon."

John turned and headed toward the temple, and Iyon toward the woods. The battle for control of Jen's mind was much more serious than she could ever realize. It could even affect her within the protection of Tolare, leaving no safe haven for Jen. Hope was doing her best to shield Jen from the onslaughts coming through a woman Jen loves. It was impossible to completely block every attack, especially if Jen would begin to seek her out on her own accord. Could Iyon help her before it was too late? He galloped into the thick of the forest in search of Jen.

....

Jen sat down on a fallen log. Normally, the birds of the air filled the forest with their music, but the songs grew silent when she drew near to them. The animals kept their distance from what they must sense to be danger lurking in the safety of their home.

Jen let herself fall into a meditative state quickly as she knew her mother would be searching for her.

Mother? I know you are out there. I can feel you. Are they hurting you?

There was pressure around Jen to stop, but she fought against it and pushed herself all the more.

Jen! Yes, I can hear you. I am fine, my darling, and I am not hurt. I am well cared for. I hope my John is well?

Before Adriana could speak further, she fell into a trance and the dragon who was secretly lurking in her mind took over the conversation, unbeknownst to Adriana.

There isn't much time for us to talk, my darling, so listen well. Hope is a traitor and Iyon is not who he says he is. They are masters of trickery and they are using you! They have great power and have twisted the real forms of the Skeign, making them look like monsters. What you see as good is bad and bad is actually good! Guard yourself! I must go, but I will be in contact with you soon and we will find a way to rescue you.

I love you Mother!

Love you as always!

The link was severed and Jen came to.

Iyon saw her sitting on the log and could feel that she had been infiltrated. Instead of letting her hear his approach, the gem glowed and Iyon lifted off the ground and floated silently in the air while trying to reach out to her.

Jen, can you hear me? Please look behind you if you can.

There was no response from Jen. Her knees were bent and pulled to her chest. With her head down and arms wrapped around her legs, Jen sat there, crying.

Iyon went up until he was directly behind her, pressed his head against her back, and gently neighed as his hooves gently touched the ground again.

Jen didn't jump away or jerk. But she felt lost and confused. Was Iyon really her enemy?

I've been looking for you.

Well, you found me.

Do you still trust me?

I can't answer that right now. Jen's eyes glazed over with tears at the sound of her own answer. What was she becoming?

There are many forces in opposition against us. Malum and Tor are after us. Hope believes all the people of Eshron to be in danger right now, the people that you helped to save.

That's not his name.

What do you mean?

Tor…that's not his name. It's Lawless. And you know, I kind of like that name, Lawless. Sounds kind of fun, don't you think?

Iyon released the bond he had with Jen and took a step back. Jen turned and faced the one she hoped beyond all shred of doubt was her real friend.

"Then it has begun. Nevertheless, I came here not to expound on the vortex. I came for other reasons. Our contact has been severed, Jen. I spoke to your mind and you could not hear me."

Tears streamed down Jen's face and she choked over her words. Her heart stabbed by the truth she could not deny, though she wanted to so badly. Was Iyon the enemy? Had he always been her enemy? She stepped off the log and turned to face him. While crying bitterly, she forced out these words. "Iyon, I understand what you're trying to do here, but you are going to have to understand that right now, I need to be left alone. I need time to think." With that, she stormed off further into the woods, leaving Iyon unable to counter the evil that was slowly taking her away. He had one plan, but it would take the help of another. Iyon turned and flew to the temple. There was still a way to save Jen from herself before it was too late.

Chapter 17
Micol

Down in the lower region of the temple buildings, a series of halls were shut off to the world. The sealed doors were locked with the source of power that emanated from within the gem that Iyon wore. Its power was needed to securely hold the most dangerous criminals. Down one of the halls in the deepest region of the temple buildings was where Celesta, the former witch queen of Eshron, was kept prisoner. She was locked in a vaulted steel cell, sealed by a force far more powerful than her own black magic.

But Iyon headed for one of the lesser halls, known as the area of disciplined confinement. These halls were also sealed by magic so there would never be a need for guards to stand watch. It was here that the guards were ordered to bring Micol and confine him until Iyon could talk with him.

Knowing Micol's capabilities, the door to his room of confinement was not locked in the regular way. It was sealed with fiery blue coils provided by Iyon himself. Not too long ago, Iyon had assembled the most talented craftsmen of Tolare. After much time, effort and experimentation, they created special artillery where Iyon could interject power that came from his eyes directly into the weapons. The soldiers could have access to that force as well. It was a groundbreaking discovery, one they intended to keep a secret until the day they would show their strength to the enemy.

Seven days had passed since Iyon left Micol to vent and fume for having been imprisoned in the temple. It did not please Iyon at all to discipline one that was like family to him. But Iyon had tried Jared's way. Time was running out, and Iyon could already foresee what would be needed. With an anxious spirit, Iyon approached the door, sealed shut by his own power. The magical blue rays that acted like bars across the door quickly retreated back into the eyes of Iyon and the door opened. Iyon entered cautiously and on guard.

The room they gave Micol was a rather large cell, at least sixteen by twelve feet in diameter, and it had everything one would need to sustain decent simple living. There was a cabinet with food, a small counter for cooking and a basin with a faucet for washing the dishes after each meal. But the room was specifically fashioned with only one plate, bowl, cup and utensils to eat and cook with. This was done so the the one being held would be forced to clean after each meal. The room was built specifically for those needing complete isolation in order to achieve a behavioral and attitude change. To Iyon's surprise, Micol had kept the place spotless. The dishes were done and put back in their proper spots and ready for their next use. Iyon let the doors lock and seal behind him. He saw Micol lying on the bed, flat on his back, repeatedly throwing a butter knife straight into the air and catching it with one hand. The bands Iyon had fastened about Micol's wrists were still in place, something that Micol promised the guards he'd find a way to pry off. What he failed to realize is they were infused with Iyon's own power, making it impossible to come off unless they were removed by Iyon alone.

"Iyon," he sarcastically pronounced. "Didn't think I'd see you here so soon. You shouldn't have even bothered to come cuz I'm not cracking. You should know once my mind is made up, there is nothing you or anyone could do to me to change it. So just go on your way, horse, you're done here."

Iyon ignored the indignant remarks. After all, Iyon was the only one that the boy had left to blame for what had happened to his father on that tragic day so long ago.

"We both lost our fathers that day, Micol. Do you think he'd want you to continue punishing yourself like this? This cannot be the end of his great legacy. I took my spot, now you must take yours."

"It's not the end of his legacy. Jared is out there. He will do just fine."

"Jared is my dear and loyal friend and fights with honor, but he was not the one born with the gifts. That came with the younger. Accept your responsibility. Take your place among the people again."

Micol sighed, obviously too overcome with his own self-pity. He tossed the knife behind him and it landed directly in the wash basin. Then he turned on his side and faced the wall.

"Just go, Iyon. I am not my father. There will never be another Captain Shan ever again. I died when he did. There's nothing more you can say to make me change my mind."

"You fought incredible battles after your father's death, not to mention your ability to kill the Skeign. You have won yourself a name to the others and they look up to you."

In a second, Micol sprang out of the bed and landed against the back wall between the basin and wash area. He crouched in attack position, faced Iyon directly and yelled, "Then why did you try to hold me back? I was killing them for him! And I don't regret for one minute my fight with you."

"Micol, you were not killing them for him. You were killing them to feed your own anger. You know that is not how we operate here. So yes, I pulled your rank from you as it was my responsibility to be your watchman, as you were to be mine. So it is pulled until you can learn to heal the proper way and let the anger go."

Iyon turned to leave.

"Don't bother coming back," retorted Micol.

"You should know, the girl you met, Jen, is in trouble, Micol. She is sinking just as you are, only worse. And she will continue to sink. Do you care about that?"

Micol shuddered and his defenses were shaken. He tried to put Jen out of his mind. The day they met had changed him. Helping her meant he would have to let the anger go. Micol teared up. But at this point it wasn't about Jen and her trouble; Micol was tearing up at the thought of releasing his anger. Without it, he was weak and vulnerable. He didn't even know who he was if he were to let it go.

"I wouldn't know how to help her," Micol admitted. "Without my anger, I don't remember who I am myself."

Iyon could sense his desperation to help Jen, so he felt confident to make the offer.

"Then I propose that you two will train together. Through that time, you will both refocus and healing will come as you help each other to release the pain. But you know the cost of your role, and she is a Key Holder. Understand the mission and the stakes here, young Captain. The bands about your wrists will remain fastened so that your whereabouts can be tracked by me. Wearing those will be your cost for freedom and your source of accountability. They will be removed when I know you are fully back with us."

Micol looked down, considering Iyon's offer. Letting out another sigh, he looked back up into Iyon's eyes, "Alright. I will agree with your proposition and I understand the terms. I will do this because of who she is. We cannot win this war without her. But I cannot say the same for me and my importance in all of this."

"Everyone is important, Micol. Don't lose sight of the need to work as one. I'm going to open this door now. Do I have your word that you will cooperate?"

"Yes, Iyon. I give you my word," Micol said solemnly back.

Sensing that some part of the old Micol was still there encouraged Iyon. The door opened and the two walked out of the room together. As they walked down the halls, doors to three other rooms opened by Iyon's will.

"Call your friends out, Micol. It is time for them to rejoin as well."

"I did not know you took them," he rebuffed.

Iyon neighed slightly, "My hand was forced, but now it is time, call them out."

"Jendal, Shek, Brendin," Micol called them with a commanding voice. It was the voice they remembered when he ruthlessly fought the Skeign creatures. It was the day he saved their lives and forever won their loyalty. They looked at Micol as they walked out of their cells and saw the new look on his face. They knew what that demeanor meant and they fell in line. Together the young group of the mighty followed Iyon out of the temple and into the light of the Tolarian sun.

Chapter 18
Passage of Time

Iyon raced through the forest to where Jen was last seen, Micol astride his back. He let the gem guide him to her. He slowed his gait and eventually came to a standstill.

"We are close. Get off and approach opposite of me. I will talk to her. You interrupt when you feel it is time to."

"Alright," Micol agreed and disappeared into the trees.

Iyon walked further into the forest as Micol made sure to steer clear of the initial altercation.

He found her deep among the trees. She was talking out loud and laughing as if she was with someone, but no one appeared to be there. He listened quietly for a moment.

"Ha ha, I can't wait for you to be here too, Mother....what's that you say...yes, there is a sky, it is the blue Tolarian sky. It goes on and on and has everything! A city, fields, forests."

Iyon's heart broke. Although Jen did not know too much, she had learned enough to be dangerous. To stop her before anything else was said, he trotted forward and called out her name as if he had not heard her talking.

"Jen, where are you?"

I have to go! I'll contact you soon, my mother!

Good bye my sweet darling!

"There you are. I've been looking for you. Please, we must talk," pleaded Iyon.

"I told you I wanted to be left alone. Why doesn't anyone listen to me around here anymore?"

"I know what your father said, but Jen, you have to listen to us before it's too late. You're slipping away and I can't save you. Do you not know that I am your true friend?"

A war between good and evil was taking place inside of her. There was a time she knew the truth and wanted nothing more than to call out to him for help, but then the other side called him a liar. The conflict within her caused her to suddenly cry out in agony. The real Jen was petrified.

"I'm begging you, Jen," Iyon persisted, "Do not listen to the voice anymore. She may sound like your mother, but Jen, she is not your mother. Don't you see that?"

Jen shook her head furiously. "No! You're wrong! Just stop talking!"

Iyon pierced Jen's soul with a sky blue ray causing Jen to stand paralyzed and her head shot back. Ever so delicately, Iyon played every memory he had of them together since the time he first found her in the field, and then more images of them in Eshron defeating the queen, her encounter with the Skeign on Shadow Earth and an image of what they had done to Iyon as he was trying to protect her in order to leave there. When he was done, he released her, leaving her shocked and without words for some time. Tears rolled down her cheeks as clouds began to lift. There was no way the Skeign could be good, which meant the voice in her head had lied to her.

"I didn't want to believe it," she whimpered, "I didn't want to believe she had been fooled. I really believed I was talking with her and for a while I was, but then her tone changed, and I knew. It's not her. It is her, but it's not."

Iyon wanted to approach Jen and comfort her, but he sensed her guard was still up against him, so he kept his distance as he talked. "At this point, I can tell you that your mother is not in any present life-threatening danger, nor is she being tortured in any way. It's more the other way around. She is voluntarily being used somehow to draw you and your father out of Tolare. When you're not under the protective covering of this place, you become vulnerable, and then you can easily be found by them. Your mind is clouded now, Jen. For they have found a way to confound you. Do you trust me now?"

"I want to," Jen cried, "But I was told not to trust you. I was told you only appear to be good." Jen stepped away as she continued to cry. The clouds in her mind were trying to come back, fighting to take back the ground that they had won inside of her.

"Then trust me, Jen."

Jen knew that voice. She turned around and saw him. It was Micol!

"Micol!" She ran to him and bear hugged him tightly. "I never got to say good bye to you earlier."

"And that's okay. I wasn't at my best, Jen. I have been running from my duties for a while, but no longer. It's time I help out with the talents I was given." That's when Jen took in the soldier clothes he was wearing, his weapons secured around his waist belt. And to add to that, it wasn't just a regular soldier's uniform. He was decorated and his clothes were that of a higher ranking officer like Fox or Jared. Jen tilted her head at the wonder of this.

He stood before her with full confidence and with tenderness in his voice as he spoke gently to her, "You know the truth; don't fight it or run from it anymore. We are your friends. Iyon is your friend and has saved your life many times. Come back to us now, Jen. Fight the darkness! And when this is over, we'll have a good laugh about all this. Deal?"

The oppression and clouds lifted again from Jen as she pushed them away, leaving her depleted of any energy she had. Still, seeing Micol was what she needed. Jen feebly looked at him and smiled, "Alright, Micol." He seemed so much like her; she felt like she could trust him.

"There you are," he chuckled and then looked at Iyon. "Iyon has a plan to help get you back on your feet. And I think it's a good one."

Iyon stepped forward and talked in a low and humble voice. "Micol will train you over the next few weeks. He doesn't have too much time to train you in combat battle. But he is the best in the art of camouflage and evading the enemy when you need to. You will use the forest for this training. And when it is time, I will call for you as we need to train together on something as well. But we cannot attempt to do that until your mind is whole again. Are you okay with this Jen?"

Jen's face beamed with a smile. For now, the clouds of evil looming in Jen's mind were gone and she could feel Iyon again.

Nothing would make me happier.

I've missed you, Jen.

And I you.

"Hope still has a plan on how to rescue your mother from the Skeign, but it is going to take a great deal of will power from you. We will address this plan in a few days' time. But first things first, Dahlia has cooked for the both of you. Climb on. I'm going to take you there the fast way."

Micol climbed on and then Jen behind him.

"Will there be lightning in the sky this time, Iyon?"

He pounced off the ground and soared through the air. "Why not?"

Iyon let the energy flow through him and then released it so fiercely that lightning filled the sky. He swiveled in and out and around the bolts as the flashes filled the sky. All the while Jen laughed tremendously knowing that she was now indeed safe among her friends.

Iyon left them alone for almost three weeks. He kept track of them as they worked in the forest, but did not show himself as Micol was keeping his part of the bargain with the serious training. Jen also had very little communication with her mother, not knowing whether or not she was being manipulated. When the thoughts came, Jen claimed that she had contracted a serious illness and was bedridden and weak. That kept the voice to a minimum as it spoke of resting and getting better soon. Jen was careful to oblige so it was not suspicious of what she was really doing.

Micol taught her how to use the forest to her advantage. They began minor sword practice with the sticks of the forest and target practice with the Taser guns which were now fueled with Iyon's mysterious blue power. Micol made sure that every minute of their time was spent wisely. He knew everything he taught her might be what she needed to save her life, and so he held nothing back. From learning camouflage and how to travel in silence, to using the trees when needed; he showed her many ways to evade the enemy. He taught her different ways a rope could be used, manipulated and knotted. And then there was the art of battle. They worked and trained until there was no energy left in either of them.

If she had not already been in good athletic shape, this rigorous schedule would have been impossible. Still, it left Jen sore and achy for the first several nights. At the end of each day, Micol accompanied her to Dahlia's and bid her a good night, all the while, making sure he did not let his emotions get in the way of what needed to be done. It was after these days with Micol that Jen was rejuvenated, feeling at peace, and more confident in herself as a fighter.

Iyon had given Jen the maximum amount of time to heal and train, but could not wait anymore, for the army was ready to leave for Eshron. Jen was all they needed to add. When Iyon pranced down the trail in the forest, he would've passed right by them had it not been for the wrist bands he used to track Micol. Iyon noticed that they were one with the forest. Jen rose from the ground and so did Micol, both wearing bushes on their backs, perfectly camouflaged. Iyon neighed delightfully.

"You blended right in with the forest, completely undetectable. Excellent work, both of you. Micol, I cannot thank you enough. You have helped Jen come back to us. But now it is my turn. Shake off those bushes, you two. We need to head to the cabin where you can wash and get a clean change of clothes and food as well. There is much to discuss and almost no time is left. Jump on."

The two climbed on his back and Iyon's heart truly rejoiced. Not only did he get Jen back, but Micol too, the son of the Captain in charge of all the armies of Tranquil Earth. He felt honored to carry them both. The gem glowed and Iyon took to the sky and in a few short minutes, they were at the cabin.

After Jen and Micol got cleaned and changed, they joined John and Dahlia around the table. Over the next hour, great fellowship mixed with delicious food. Spirits were high and Jen stored and cherished the moments in her heart. She could hardly believe they were getting ready for war. She pushed that thought aside, not wanting anything to ruin this special occasion. After lunch was over, Jen embarked with Iyon on a training mission of their own. Deep in the woods, Iyon stood with Jen on his back; they were completely alone.

"Jen, in order to survive the next mission; you're going to need to open and close portals within seconds of one another while I run at my top speed. They don't need to be big openings. I only need one large enough for me to jump through. All you need to do is stay connected to the ancient river that flows from the Chest and let it work through you. Without that connection, we won't make it."

Thinking too much about it instead of surrendering and letting the power do its work was always the hardest part for Jen. But she did have experience in Shadow Earth with combining locations of travel through thought. She was grateful for that practice.

"Remember, the ancient forces that run through you will work as long as you remain focused and do not give in to darker thoughts. So we're going to try this form of travel here in Tolare. We won't be leaving Tolare at all, so you will not need to fear anything regarding that."

Jen breathed in deeply. "Okay, Iyon. I think I'm ready. Let's give this a try."

As soon as Jen raised her hand level with the ground, there was no hesitation. The energy surged through her and shot an opening a few yards from them. Iyon pounced through it and in seconds they were near the temple. But they did not stop there. Over the course of the next several minutes, Jen and Iyon had transported from the temple to the army camps, from the camps to the forest, to Dahlia's, and then the fields. Finally, they ended at the temple as their final destination. Jen was invigorated and confident. Once again, she felt at one with the Warrior Horse while sitting on his back. Iyon proudly pranced to the platform in the center of the temple and the two were lowered down into the deep abyss to converse with Hope.

By now the armies had left camp and were approaching the fields' just south-west of the temple. They marched as one, dressed for battle. Forthcoming wars and fierce battles were on the horizon. It was in the air. Everyone could sense its imminent arrival.

Chapter 19
The Message from Hope

There in the abyss, the great tree hung in the air. The blackness vanished as the bark once again split down the center and spread apart, revealing Hope's wondrous glows. Off to her right was the Chest, resting freely on its own floating platform. It was a perplexing sight. Something about this scene seemed unreal, yet here she was and it was very real. A gentle heat radiated from the Chest and filled every part of Jen's being. At that point she knew that this was good. The lies spoken to her by the enemy through her own mother were inevitably exposed as the light brought clarity, making her feel secure.

Jen.

It spoke in unison as Hope and the Being from within the Ancient River Chest spoke to her heart. The immensity of the power caused Jen to drop to her knees and she began to shake.

I'm here.

It is true, Jen. They are using your mother, Adriana, against you as you now have experienced firsthand. If you continue to succumb to their will, the less union you will have with us. The River you feel cannot ride through one who is divided.

Tears stained Jen's face as she knew they spoke the truth. Now Hope talked alone.

"We have discussed how to keep your mother alive until she can be rescued. As long as she proves useful to the enemy, they will continue to treat her decently. So let's have them think that their plan with you is working. What you will need to do is no easy task. If you want to preserve her safety you will need to continue talking with her. They will begin to ask for details on plans once you commit to them. We will give you false plans and when they are busy chasing phantoms, we will launch the rescue attempt. Will you be able to do this?"

Lying to her mother in order to save her life cut Jen deeply, but it did prove to be the most logical play at the time.

"It seems like a crazy plan, Hope, but a good one. I will agree to act like I believe her and let them think they have won me over. But I don't think this will last long at all. We will need to move fast."

"We will commence with plans for your mother after the rescue mission for the people of Eshron. Her people are in trouble and that situation must be handled first and foremost. As I prepare to address the people of Tolare, your father has asked that he be the one to tell you what you and Iyon must do to make that happen. I will see you all in a moment."

Iyon nodded his head and the platform they were standing on rose to the top. A platform above them moved away and allowed them through until they were once again standing in the temple courts.

Zurina, dressed in full combat clothes, walked up to Jen, who still sat on Iyon's back.

"Jen, come with me. I have brought you clothes for this mission. You must change quickly."

Jen slid off Iyon's back and followed Zurina into an inner room, where Jen found the warrior uniform she wore when she rescued her father, freshly cleaned and ready for another mission. However, this time there were more weapons included. Lying next to the artillery was her father's backpack. Jen looked at it and wondered.

"Your father wanted you to have it for today. He adjusted the straps so that it could fit tightly on your back and keep your hands free. He also emptied out the contents. It's now filled with items that you worked with during your training with Micol. And a birr fruit is in there, of course."

"Thanks, Zurina, for everything you've done for me."

"It's what I'm meant to do."

"Keep an eye out for my dad, would you?"

"With my life."

Zurina turned to leave, but motioned to the small samurai sword lying on the other bed.

"The uniform now has a place for you to safely lodge the sword tightly against your back, giving you the ability to grab it with your right hand. The holster for the hand Taser will be to your left side. Let the handmaids help you with that. It's their job to make sure your weapons and uniform are without flaws."

Over the next couple of minutes, Jen got dressed. Then two handmaids entered the room. One made sure that everything was put into position while the other put Jen's hair up and pinned it tight. She left the room and entered back into the courtyard where she found Zurina and Dahlia. Jen took notice that everyone was standing outside of the temple; no one was standing under the dome. She looked across the way and saw her father. He was standing next to Jared, Micol, Fox and Taq. He too was dressed for battle; it was the first time she had ever seen her father dressed like that.

Iyon walked to the center of the temple and stood silently. All small talk came to an abrupt halt as everyone turned their attention to the stallion. Iyon reared up and neighed powerfully. As his hooves hit the floor, the ringer of the bells began his job as Iyon gallantly strode out of the temple area. The bells were heard throughout all of Tolare. Those that were inside came hurrying out of their homes or places of work and looked in the direction of the temple. Any working the fields or gardens stopped and did the same, all waiting. The soldiers who filled the fields to the south-west of the temple fell swiftly and silently into rows of perfect formation. All from the town turned toward the temple and waited with great anticipation.

Jen?

Dad! How is that you are in my mind?

I have melded with the Chest as well, my daughter. We are both needed at the same time in different places. I will tell you right now, my mission and the success of it depends solely on your success. Do you remember all our training together on the locations of the worlds of Earth, the pictures I had you memorize and the other worlds?

Yes, I can remember those places clearly.

Good, you will need to be completely focused for this mission and be able to travel to those places. You and Iyon must be the decoy to distract Malum and the vortex while we are busy in Eshron. You may need to act as if you are looking for something or are on an important mission in order to keep him off our scent. If they detect what we are doing, then they could decide to come for us and many lives could be lost. This is a dangerous mission for both of us. Know that I love you, daughter, and we both must do what we are called to do.

I love you too, Father and I am ready for this. We will do our very best to distract them.

We will move quickly — above all, you must stay absolutely focused. Stay in tune with the River and you will be okay.

I will, Father. I promise.

Now look toward the temple. The spectacular event you are about to witness may never be equaled again.

The platform began to spin and moved beneath the earth. Those present intently waited for what was to come next. All of Tolare, including the animals were silent.

The pillars of the temple groaned and creaked as it stretched and elongated itself, lifting the ceiling high into the sky and then the pillars and dome became transparent. The floor opened up further and out from the black abyss arose the floating tree. The leafless branches became visible, vibrating and quivering under the natural desire to grow life from its limbs. The tree kept rising until it was positioned high above the temple platform. The awe-inspiring sight of the roots whipping around in mid-air caused all the people to shield their eyes for what was to come. Instantaneously, the trunk split apart as light burst forth from the tree. The portal emerged from within the tree; it was as circular as the sun and displayed all the colors of the rainbow. Suddenly, buds popped out on all the branches and just like watching time speed forward, beautiful large green leaves of all shapes and sizes grew and lavishly swayed in the Tolarian breeze. This all happened right before their eyes.

There was no other place Jen would rather be than right where she was, at the foot of this massive tree, blazing with brilliance stronger than the sun. As the intensity of the light faded, people stopped shielding their eyes and waited for Hope to speak.

"People of Tolare, I greet you." Hope's voice carried throughout all of Tolare. No matter how far one of the townspeople was from the temple, from the closest person to the person farthest away, everyone heard equally.

"It has been refreshing to have experienced a season of healing under the safety of the Great Covering which protects our home from invasion. I have come to tell you that our enemies are organizing, and tumultuous times of trouble and chaos are coming for all the worlds of Earth. We knew from when time began that there would be a season where darkness would have its reign. The dawn of the day for that season is now upon us. Deployments of troops are being sent to Eshron for their protection against a ruthless foe that has risen up. Those that remain must train and prepare for future missions. Those that have been assigned to housing will begin to raise new structures as more refugees will be pouring into Tolare.

"The dawn of darkness is now upon us. Our enemy will soon acquire all he needs to throw True Earth into utter chaos. I will tell you this now. Do not be surprised if it appears that our enemies have won this war. Do not be surprised at the destruction they cause. For at the culmination when evil is at its highest; it will be utterly destroyed and cleansed forever! We will survive; we will make it through these perilous times!"

Thousands of fists raised in the air all across Tolare as the people shouted cheers. The determination to survive no matter the situation was set in stone in the hearts of those that thrived in Tolare. For all who had survived and been given the blessing of living within its protection knew in their hearts that one day, they would be called to fight, to serve, and use their talents in order to save as many as could be saved during the terrible days that lie ahead.

As Hope started to retreat back into the tree, she left them with these parting words. "I call on you now to be strong, take courage, and above all, never give up your hope. Hang on until the end has come. That is what I must ask of you. We will commence into action starting from this day forward. Be strong now, Tolarians, be strong!"

At the end of her words, a strong breeze blew into the temple; the leaves on the great floating tree broke off with ease and were carried away by the strength of the wind. They blew over the hill, and past the woods; then magically, like fireflies filling a night sky, they each burst into white glowing flames and vanished. The great tree was barren again. As the crowd chanted and cheered Hope retreated completely into the trunk. It closed and sealed her in as the tree lowered back into the black abyss. The circular platform moved over the hole, sealing all light from the abyss. The pillars of the temple reappeared as it creaked and groaned once again and it shrank back to its original shape.

Immediately, the people of Tolare went to work, each knowing their role in helping to build the city up and preparing it for the arrival of those in need of its saving grace.

"It is time for us to join the troops!" a tall man standing near John commanded. His uniform was more intricately detailed, particularly the golden star that rested prominently on the right side of his chest.

Jen leaned toward Iyon and murmured, "Who is that man there, standing by my father?"

"That is General Stantyon, a war hero with scars branded across his body to prove his battle worth. He will accompany your father and is a man you can trust with your father's life. That is why he is going."

The group left the temple and briskly walked down the hill to where the troops stood in perfect formation, at attention and ready for action. Jen saw that even Zurina was among the ones going to Eshron. Jen smiled at the fortitude and strength of that woman, knowing full well she would not hesitate to take any opportunity presented to serve and protect Eshron.

Jen stood on the hill with Iyon, overlooking the mass of troops ready to deploy. Knowing there was no way to say good bye to her special friend or thank him for helping her; she whispered out loud instead, "Be safe,

Micol."

"When we have more time, I will tell you the stories of the boy you have run into. But for now, know that you need not worry about his safety. He is ranked in Tolare as one of the finest warriors. His blood runs thick with that of his father's."

Jen was taken aback at Iyon's words. "For his age, how is that possible?"

"Because he is a prodigy." Iyon turned and walked to the building next to the outdoor temple. "Come, Jen," he called to her. "They will be deploying in the next hour or so and that doesn't leave us much time to prepare for what we must accomplish."

Jen? Are you well? I'm getting so concerned as we haven't talked.

Don't worry, Mother, I am formulating a plan to get you. Hope does not want me to leave Tolare, but I promise you that I will. I will come for you soon! I have decided to believe you. I could not talk too much for the past couple of weeks as they had me guarded. They don't trust me anymore. So I have decided firmly to come to you. Do you have any ideas of how I can get to you?

I do, my daughter. Perhaps we will finally be together! I will tell you where you can go that you will be safe.

Men are approaching again. I will be in touch with you soon.

Until then.

After Jen finished her private talk, she gazed at the mass below her one last time with a look of pride and determination, and then hurried to be by Iyon's side. The two disappeared into the temple buildings and began their own preparations.

Chapter 20
The Mission

It was to be a coordinated effort. Jen and Iyon would take off first as decoys to lure Malum and Tor after them. Whether Jen wanted it or not, Hope had her eat a birr fruit, just in case they were delayed by a few days.

Iyon was breathing rapidly, gearing up to start at a dead run. Jen sat confidently on his back, holding on to nothing more than his mane. Her veins pulsated and her head was clear for the mission.

"Give them as much time as you possibly can. Two days, if possible."

Jen and Iyon nodded, both ready for the race.

Have you picked out a lineup of locations across the worlds? Iyon asked in her mind.

I do, I have thirty specific locations. When things get bad at one, I'll be ready for the next in line.

Remember this, Jen. If Malum should get too close to me or if anything happens, promise me you will separate yourself from me. Get to a safe place so that if I am in need of help, you can always come back for me.

I promise I will.

Ready?

I'm ready. Let's do this! The Contana Fields of the Elm World.

Jen raised her hand, the power flowed, Iyon reared with a tremendous war cry neigh and they pounced through the portal.

. . . .

The thick brush of this world was taller than Iyon. They were running at a dead pace for a few paces but Iyon slowed to a quick walk. He let the gem fuse with his own strength until it lifted his hooves off the ground so as not to leave a trail.

"This....was a good idea. These fields stretch for miles and miles. We can make good distance from our entrance point and it will take longer for them to find us."

After several minutes of Iyon skating above the ground, he came to an abrupt halt in the thickest brush possible. He reclined in a lying down position, but remained floating in case they needed to make a fast break for it. The tall stalks of grass around them towered a clear ten feet above them. Jen thought of her survival skills she had learned from Micol and grabbed the stalks closest to them. Taking string from her father's bag, she cleverly intertwined it through the stalks. Now when the wind blew, the grass would still sway but not expose their cover. The winds shifted direction and an eerie presence covered the land.

It's the vortex; it's looking for us.

For the next hour, the vortex furiously stormed over the fields. It became so impatient it would suck the grass up like a vacuum, leaving nothing but the plain dirt. The wind died down and for a moment, Jen thought they were in the clear.

"Iyon! I know you are in these fields. Surrender yourself, and I'll let the girl live."

Jen.

Just tell me when.

I'm going to make a break for it after I talk to him.

"Leave us be, Malum! We have many sick in Tolare and need supplies."

Lawless started to fly toward them. Iyon flew out at lightning speed.

Now!

As one, Jen pictured her next destination and Iyon jumped through the portal with the vortex at his back hooves, barely escaping capture.

As Iyon jumped through to the other side, he did not alter his speed. It was the entrance to the underground Rocky Maze of the Darth world. The series of paths that continued for miles underground were shrouded in complete darkness. There were thousands of turns with many dead ends.

"Another wise choice! I know these mazes well; my father trained me here when I was a colt. I had forgotten about this place. We can keep them at bay for a while here!"

"My father had these all picked out when I studied with him, it's like he knew this was exactly what I needed to know in order to survive."

"He is a smart man indeed. I hope they are doing well now."

"Well, let's give them as much time as we can," Jen concluded.

Iyon charged boldly into the maze, knowing exactly where every dead end was and which ones would get him to an opening on the other side of the mountains, so he raced at a furious pace in hopes of staying ahead of the vortex. Far behind them, the sounds of blasts and thunder tore through the maze. They were angering it, as it was becoming obsessed with wanting to win this cat and mouse game. Jen and Iyon had succeeded in sucking it into their trap, at least for now.

Chapter 21
Divisions

Only thirty minutes after Jen and Iyon left, a section of the army under Taq, the acting Captain, headed through the portal which John had created that led straight into the city of Eshron. Micol had been given the responsibility of determining the first round of people to come out of the city. With his legendary past, his comrades were eager to see him back in position and with a sound mind. It helped the morale of the entire army. The soldiers under him were his three friends, along with almost one hundred others. Their job was to help the first wave with packing up wagons, loading up supplies on the backs of horses and donkeys and moving out.

Taq and the men under him went into the houses with the remaining people and helped them finish packing. The people of the city moved at a rapid pace, having been quietly forewarned by Hope's earlier message. Realizing the threat of evil that could attack them, they packed their personal belongings during the night, with windows closed and lights to a minimum. No one dared to mention the evacuation during the light of day for fear that the one they knew as Tor could be watching or listening to their conversations. So the people moved about as normal during the day and prepared quietly by night. When the troops came, bags were ready with supplies and household goods. The people had cleverly hid them away in closets, under beds or in cabinets. Micol and his men carried out their job fast and with efficient precision so that within the hour, the first round of supplies with women, children and the elderly were being ushered safely into Tolare. Then Taq and his men moved quickly with the next round of evacuees.

John remained at the portal gate with a band of guards around him as he held his hand steady to keep the portal open as wagons, people, and herds of animals were ushered through. And that's when he felt it again. The presence; he knew who it was that was calling him. Only this time, he answered.

What is it, Adriana?

All this time! You knew it was me and yet you war against me? How I have missed you! And now, you finally reach out to me. What horrible thing have they turned you into?

How was I to know you were abetting the enemy?

Liel is not our enemy. He is kind and gentle to me.

You should test that theory of yours. Tell him no just once and watch the monster he will become.

There's that man of science I know! Always wanting to test your silly theories.

Not so silly when they prove themselves to be true. Tell me, where are you now?

I'm lying in a soft bed that is covered with red satin sheets and trimmed with pure gold. I wish you could be here with me, but you fight for the enemy and don't even know it.

It is you who is being deceived. Do you really think the Skeign are good creatures, or is that something you have to tell yourself every time you open your eyes and become a slave for your Master?

He is not my Master!

He's not, how can you be so sure?

It is true, John. Every time I wake up I tell myself that they are good and what you fight for is not, but what else can I do? This is where I am, so this is how I must be to survive. You left me, remember? What else was I supposed to do?

Adriana! You have sacrificed your conscience? For what? And then you put the guilt on me? You do what is right, no matter the cost. That is what you are supposed to do.

Would you rather he kill me?

No! Of course not. I have been trying to find a way to rescue you. But you have to trust me again, Adriana. I am the one that loves you. Do you trust me?

Yes. I do.

Then let me help you.

Please, John. Get me out of here! I'm so tired.

I will. You will need to tell me where you are. I need clues to find you.

I will gather clues next time we talk. I know the realm we live in is secured. The only one I see enter and leaving is Liel himself.

Then find the door from which he comes and goes, and describe that door to me. I have to go. I will get you to safety.

I love you!

I love you too, my Adriana.

John continued to stand quietly in position and said nothing of his altercation to the others. It was a double standard, telling his daughter to not engage with her, yet here he was, fraternizing with the enemy. But she was his wife. No matter what, John would make every attempt to rescue her and not stop until she was safe. He did not intend to keep his talk with her a secret, but he would speak to the right audience when the time was right. The desire to be reunited with his wife burned within his soul.

Hang in there, Adriana, just a little more. I will come for you!

. . . .

Dodging and twisting small pathways, using only the light of the gem fastened on Iyon's breastplate as their single light source, they spent hours in the maze. Feeling confident that they had completely confounded the vortex long enough, Iyon found the pathway that led out. Thundering hard, they finally saw it; the light at the end of the tunnel. Never before had Jen been so grateful to see light. The darkness was confining and she could not wait to move onto their next target destination.

As soon as we breach the light, let's make our exit. What do you have in mind next?

Back to the Elm world and into the dark lands. I still want them to think we were getting something from there.

They were seconds from breaching the light.

Jen raised her hand and the portal outside the tunnel began forming.

As soon as Iyon exited the darkness, he leaped into the air, ready for their next destination, and then everything for him went black.

The force of the blow that had struck Iyon in the right temple and the other force that struck his neck caused Iyon to flip to the right; Jen was ejected off his back and flew through the air. In a split second she created a portal and fell through it before being dashed against rocks. Iyon's body slammed to the ground and didn't move.

Jen fell back into the fields of the Contana, where she had thought was the safest place to land without being wounded. She fell to the ground and rolled out into a standing position. She stood there for just a moment, fighting to catch her breath as shock tried to take over. She shook it off and refocused.

I won't lose control, not this time!

With a warrior determination and a will to not give up, Jen thought of the mounds around where Iyon had fallen, and formed the portal. Quietly, she walked through and hid among the rocks. She had entered the world where they had exited the cave, only on the ledge above. She looked down and braced herself to be ready if Malum had successfully killed Iyon.

Iyon was lying still on his side, not moving. It looked as if Malum was using his own evil source of power which thundered through his eyes and was continuing to press into Iyon's face and neck.

The vortex blew a hole through the wall and looked down on their prize. "Finally! What trouble this one gave me. So, to the Witch's Abyss with him?"

"Yes, I will do unto him what was done to me. After this day, Iyon will be no more."

"And what of the girl?"

"She has become extremely good at portal shifting. She escaped. But she will turn up. But for now, we have a great prize to give to the witches. The Last Warrior Guardian will be theirs. Let's go!"

Tor scooped up Iyon's body with Malum following right behind. They disappeared into the vortex, leaving Jen alone. Jen screamed into the mountain air. She picked up rocks and threw them as hard as she could while screaming Iyon's name over and over again. Finally, she dropped to her knees and continued to wail. How in all the worlds of Earth and beyond would she ever find where they were taking him?

Then a name came into her mind. *Celesta. You will know of this Witch's Abyss.*

Jen wiped her tears and created a portal that took her straight to the temple of Tolare. Her blood pumped with an iron will that would not bend. She would not rest until he was secured, dead or alive.

. . . .

Malum and Iyon were transported to the lair of the witches. Iyon was placed directly on the altar surrounded by many black-hooded witches. On the large altar were three poles made of white liquid metal and fortified with centuries' worth of witchcraft, spells and incantations. Iyon was transported within the triangle of poles. Its liquid chains reached out and wrapped around his hooves, face, and breastplate, all the while, the witches repeated the same spell over and over again while swaying side to side. Next to the altar stood a golden pedestal with a bowl-shaped top. The witches' swaying intensified and their chants became louder as the witch mother of them all came out from a side room and walked into their sanctuary. In her wrinkled hands she carried a white glowing orb. Walking over to the pedestal, she placed the orb in the bowl and stood in front of Iyon. She raised her hands in the air and all incantations stopped.

Malum was watching from the rear of the room, remembering back to the day when the transformation had happened to him. He wished Iyon was conscious to feel the death of his own soul. It would have been the perfect revenge. But his death and resurrection as his own personal servant committing murder and destruction for the next millennium would be equally pleasing to Malum, so he stood there, content just to watch.

The witch mother of them all began her recitation. "Daughters of my craft, we are gifted by our son, Malum, whom we created long ago to be our faithful one. He has this day brought us a great prize. Behold, the last Warrior Guardian of all the worlds of Earth! With his death, the power of evil sways the scales in the favor of our Father. Let the transformation of his soul begin!"

At the end of the recitation, the room burst forth with loud wails and cries as the witches fell into trances. The evil magic filled the room and Iyon's soul began to drain from his body as it was slowly and methodically sucked into the cursed white poles.

Chapter 22
Plans and Supplications

The fields near the Tolarian temple were filled with the people from Eshron. The Tolarians were hard at work, putting up tents and bringing in supplies. Tents were pitched, fires were started and caldrons for cooking stews were brought as garden foods from the farms of Tolare poured into the camp. Water jugs were filled from the springs. In a matter of hours, the population of Tolare increased dramatically. The entire camp bustled with the task of becoming adjusted to what they hoped would not be their new way of life, but just a temporary safe haven until the danger was over in Eshron.

The last caravan arrived, led by John, meaning they had completed the evacuation mission successfully. As soon as the last group came through, the portal closed; Taq, Micol, General Stantyon and John began making their way to the temple. And that's when Jen's portal appeared up near the top of the hill by the outer temple court. They looked in pleasant surprise as it was formed and waited in great anticipation to see the two victors come forth. Jen stepped through the portal and let it close behind her. She wanted to honor Iyon with her strength, so she stood strong, holding back her tears. She turned her pale face toward the approaching group of men. Their smiles vanished as they saw the desperate expression upon her face. The commotion at the temple came to a halt and John and the others quickened their pace to reach Jen. Her eyes were fixated on her father as he approached her. She did not move until they were directly in front of her. With people already whispering their concern, everyone near to Jen kept their voices to a minimal.

John put his hand on her shoulder, "Let's go down and talk with Hope right away. Best not to say anything here and cause a widespread panic."

The group walked to the center platform. Despite no one placing their foot where Iyon normally pounded his hoof into the stone, the circular floor immediately lowered, giving everyone the feeling that Hope knew what had happened to Iyon already.

Down in the abyss, the trunk to the magical tree had already split into its oval shaped form and Hope's colors of sadness, rays of deep yellow flashed across the room.

As soon as the group was level with Hope; Jen bravely stepped forward, gathered her strength and explained in detail the events that had ended in Iyon's capture. She finished, "And I didn't even know if Iyon was dead or alive." With quivering lips, Jen's head hung low as she let the tears flow.

The group stood silent, no one knowing what to do, as the thought of proceeding in the war without Iyon was utterly unimaginable. After all, it was through him that they had all found their way to Tolare. It was he who had fought the battles with the Skeign and had defeated them time after time. Now, without his steadfast strength and encouragement, what would they become? John finally broke the silence.

"Hope, do you sense his presence anywhere?"

"I have been searching for his presence and I do not feel him anywhere. That only happens when a Warrior falls. Their presence within me disappears."

"Hope, that's not true," blurted out Jen.

"Jen, I am connected with all Warriors. It is how I keep track of all their whereabouts and outcomes."

"I understand what you say, but Malum was very specific. He said that he was going to do to Iyon what was done to him. Iyon wouldn't be dead if that were so. Do you know where the Witch's Abyss is? We can invade it and retrieve Iyon."

"I've never heard of this 'Witch's Abyss,' nor would I know how to find it," Hope sadly admitted.

"Then we go and talk to the one that probably does. Allow us access to Celesta," Jen demanded. "She's the only one that can help us at this point."

Hope became sullen. Using evil to find good was an abomination to her, but she knew there was little choice here.

"Let it be done then," she surrendered.

Within moments the platform rose to the surface and the group ran toward the passageway that led to the inner temple confinement rooms. Celesta's was the furthest underground and it would take time to get through the security doors held closed by Iyon's own doing.

Like clockwork, they used the weapons Iyon fashioned to retract his power from the bolted doors, and then unlocked the manual bolts next. One door after the other, the company made their way deeper and deeper down into the earth to find the witch queen. As each felt the growing dread of Iyon's possible outcome but refusing to admit it, they moved all the faster until they reached the vault; an iron box with coils of blue electricity wrapped dozens of times around it. There was one intercom for the vault so one could talk to the prisoner. But that too was protected by blue rays of energy so that Celesta could pull no tricks. Its only purpose was for communication.

Cautiously, they all approached the cell of the witch.

. . . .

The roaring voices of the enchantments were now accompanied by those playing drums with drumsticks molded from the bones of the dead. They were pounding away on skulls as all chanted to the sound of the drummers' beat. The witch mother swayed side to side as the poles fully increased with power, glowing with such a blinding light that the witches could barely stand. There was nothing Iyon could do this time. His soul was overcome and his last breath came as the living poles of pure wickedness drained his power down to nothing. As the Mother saw him draw his last breath, she raised her fists into the air. All drumming and chanting came to an immediate halt. All that was heard in the room was the exhale of Iyon's last breath.

"It is done!"

Those holding staffs began a cadence, hitting the ground slowly as the witch mother pointed to the orb upon the pedestal.

"Now, entomb him forever!"

With the pounding of the staffs, the chains released Iyon's body and floated to the orb, wrapping around it. The energy and soul of Iyon was sent into it until every last bit of life source had seeped out of the chains and into the eternal prison. With their work complete, the chains fell flat on the ground, as if they were never alive to begin with. They then turned black, followed by the poles.

The witch mother approached the orb, which glowed fiercely and looked as if there was an electrical storm and a fierce ocean raging on the inside. She placed her hands around it, picked it up and stepped in front of them all. Raising the orb triumphantly above her head, she proclaimed. "Here lies the last and greatest Warrior. May his soul never rest in peace!"

The choir of witches cheered at their accomplishment. It had taken all their power to destroy Iyon. They were sweating profusely from exhaustion, but still, they continued to cheer. It was during their sadistic celebration that a rickety old witch who wore chains about her body came out and stood in front of them. The chains that were wrapped around her bound her to another orb, black as a starless night and carried with it a putrid smell.

The witch mother, who was now leaning on a staff that was given to her for support, held up her hand again. "Settle down, my children! We have yet one more job to do. The day has come for us to spawn another gelding for our Malum. We will use this empty body to create a son for him, someone he can train for the days of evil ahead. But first, let us replenish our strength and draw from the source that continues to faithfully empower us, for we are far too weak to take on this great task."

Slowly the witches kneeled and lowered their faces to the ground. The room fell silent. Malum remained standing in the rear and then slowly backed out of the room. When he was a safe distance away from the witches, he called for Tor who had slipped away. Shortly, the vortex reappeared.

"I want to go to Eshron while we are waiting for the witches to recover their strength. It's time to fill the prisons we have created for the doomed."

"Malum, we should seek another land."

"I don't want another land! I want those people to pay. Now take me there."

"As you wish," the vortex abruptly said and whisked Malum away to Eshron.

Chapter 23
The Price to Pay

Jen approached the metallic box and made her way to the intercom. Her heart raced, her hands shook and she needed to control her ragged breathing. She took a few breaths to gain her composure and regain strength to speak to the witch.

"Celesta."

A seductive, evil laugh came from within the cell.

"So, why does a great Key Holder come down to see a witch? Something you need, perhaps?"

"Quit playing your games with us," John demanded. "The Witch's Abyss, you will tell us where it is or we will see to it that your prison box will become half the size it is now."

"My, my my," Celesta sang the words seductively. "You must be the father I've heard so much about. Such a threat can only be accomplished by the power of Iyon. Tell me, dear John; where is Iyon now? Perhaps if he asks me I would gladly cooperate."

"He is busy right now."

"No, John; you're lying…You should never lie to a witch. We can tell, you know."

She laughed maniacally again.

"Your Iyon is dead. I can feel my sisters now. They have done their job. Leave me! I do not care what you do to me. I will not give my sisters up.

The scale has tipped in our favor. Soon, Tor will come for me and free me from this cell. I will rejoin my sisters and you all will perish!"

Lightning flashed inside the cell. It vibrated and shook from the power trapped inside of it. Celesta screamed in a torturous rage, begging to be released from the cell but she wasn't talking to Jen or the others. She whimpered and then her body collapsed to the ground.

The others turned to leave quietly, shaking their heads at the time they had wasted. Jen approached the intercom and said, "Celesta, if Tor ever comes for you, he will destroy you. You kept him trapped when you knew how to free him. Malum freed Tor and told him of your selfishness. That vortex will never be your friend again."

Jen waited for a response but she was only answered with silence. She got up to leave, despairing that her plan did not work.

"Only through Tor could I ever go home…now…he will kill me instead. He will kill me instead."

Jen whipped around and stared at the others, and then broke into a sprint, passing them without saying a word.

Come on! I know what to do; she called to her father's mind.

"Catch up to her," John said. The others sprang into a dead sprint in pursuit of Jen.

She called out to them to run faster, as the plan to save Iyon spurred her on until she came to the outer temple and stood right where Iyon would slam his hoof down on the circular stone platform. The others caught up with her and walked onto the platform.

The group kept quiet until the platform lowered itself and became level with Hope. Jen could contain her excitement no more.

"I know how we can find Iyon."

"She cooperated?" Hope questioned.

"Not exactly. But I know what I must do. I need to contact Tor, and only Tor. There is something I learned from William's journals and I believe I know how to lure it to me so that I can surrender to it. We need to get the vortex without Malum interfering."

"What!" John interrupted. "Jen, I thought you said you had a plan.

How is that a plan?"

"Dad, it was the vortex that took your great grandfather. It was William who betrayed Tor and left it to languish in the tunnels. I can contact it as a direct descendant of William's family and taunt it to come to me so that it can have its revenge. I'll beg for forgiveness. I can say that I will go without a fight if I can say my final good bye to Iyon. If he does not consent, then I will step back into my portal and the plan will have failed. But that vortex has no allegiance to anything. I think it will fall for the trap."

"How is that a trap? Even if he does and you walk through, you will be a prisoner."

"No I won't. I'm feeling within me something can be done. Something incredibly unexpected," she paused and looked at the chest. Her heart palpitated strong as waves of heat tremored fiercely through her veins. "I need a moment."

Just then, a platform rose up from the deep abyss and Jen walked onto it. The others stayed where they were as Jen was taken to where the Chest sat. A pounding sound similar to a heartbeat came from within the Chest as Jen drew near. Stepping onto its platform, she walked up to it, bent down on one knee; placed her hands on its sides and opened it up.

. . . .

We are in a place known as Liel's Earth, John. Can you hear me? It used to be known as Free Earth, but he has taken it over.

And how do I know this is my Adriana?

Because…you were right, I overheard Liel talking. He means to kill me now that something that he needs has been released. I do not think you will have time to get to me before he does.

Adriana cried, and then regained her strength to talk.

I don't want you to come after me, but I do want you to know where to find me when this is all over. Within his castle that is deep underground, there is a large red door that he enters through. No one else is allowed through the door except him. Perhaps there is a way to blast through the door and get to me. I am on the other side of it. Do not come after me, John. I have to live with the mistake I made. I love you, my dear. Fight hard and always know that my love for you is true.

I love you, too.

John was shaken. His face paled as desperation to rescue her now more than ever filled his heart. It was time. Whether she wanted him to or not, it was time.

The river burst out of the chest and picked Jen up. The waves of light danced in the air as it communed with Jen. John and the others marveled at the sight.

. . . .

Malum walked among the empty streets of Eshron, both stunned and impressed at Iyon's stealth move. It was a clever decoy on Iyon's part, but one that would cost him an eternal life of imprisonment while his body would be used for destruction.

Malum continued to walk through the town until he reached the castle at the far end. The vortex appeared next to Malum. "He tricked me. They could've all belonged to me but you had me wait." Malum could feel the spite against him.

"He tricked us both. Eshron will still pay. Level this city down to nothing. Let not one stone be left on top of another!"

The vortex was hesitant to listen, but acted nonchalant. It really didn't understand its place among the worlds, yet it wanted to be no one's servant. Here it was, listening to a being far lower than itself. It would not have listened to Malum, if it did not feel like destroying something. For now, the destruction of a city seemed appealing.

Tor rose up in strength and power. The winds churned until it looked no different than the fiercest of tornados. It lifted from the ground and began pounding the city buildings. It moved slowly, making sure that every building was reduced to rubble.

. . . .

Jen was carefully lowered by the dancing light until she was standing upon her own platform. The lights moved back into the chest and the lid closed by itself. As the platform momentarily connected with the other, Jen stepped off and rejoined the group; the appearance of her face looked as if it were slightly glowing from having been with the Ancient.

"I need to leave the city. When I do, I will call Lawless to me. I will stay connected with the river throughout this time. If he takes me to the Witch's Abyss, then as I am passing through it, I will create a vortex of my own. There is a way to trap it. At that time the army will pass through the portal and attack the witches. They will never see this coming."

Jared nodded his head in approval. "Now that….is a good plan. I will call a few units to attention to depart immediately. We will retrieve Iyon back."

And this is when John saw his moment.

"When they are attacked, there will be a distraction in the forces of evil. Liel as the Head should become confused and weakened. I want to launch an attack of my own at the same time. I know where Adriana is. Hope, they are going to kill her. Now is the time. I have to try, or die trying."

Jen was stunned at the words out of his mouth. She couldn't move or speak. The emotions that swirled within her heart felt like a painful eruption of deadly arrows.

"Dad!" she mumbled, "She works for the enemy."

"She was deceived by him, yes. But I know where she is. She and others from Earth are on Free Earth." He turned his attention to the one that needed to grant him permission.

"Hope, I won't be much use to you or this war if I don't try now. My strength will drain and I will be a worthless man if I don't fight for my wife when I am given the chance. I give you my word, if I am overcome; I will make a portal and evacuate without her. You made a promise to me long ago that every attempt would be made to rescue my wife. Now it's time to grant me permission to go."

Hope cast a wave across the room full of energy and full of sorrow. She knew that John would have to go, but his final outcome remained unsure.

"Free Earth was destroyed many seasons ago. I have searched for it. Liel took it a long time ago," said Hope.

"He didn't destroy it. He merely perverted its essence and then hid it from all known dimensions to keep it as his safe haven. It's his lair and that's where he's keeping her. With a decoy plan of my own, I have a chance."

"I can see that if I do not let you do this, then you will never forgive yourself, nor will I be able to live with myself. You're right, I made you a promise and so this must be carried out. We will launch an attack on two fronts at the same time. Our enemy will not suspect this. John's company of men that go with him must be minimal, but strong and mighty."

Hope turned her attention to the men standing near, quietly and patiently. "General Stantyon, Jared, and Taq; pull your units together and go with John. Micol, you will take two hundred strong and go with Jen. Destroy every witch in sight. None can be left alive or else they will send word to Liel. This blow to the force of evil will send a trickle effect all the way to his lair. He will not know where it is coming from. Make use of every weapon Iyon has put his energy into so that you all can have a chance. So let it be done."

The platform immediately rose and the group was soon standing in the outer temple courts with the Tolarian sun bathing their faces. Within the next hour, two very deadly attacks would be launched and the outcome of both would be either victorious or catastrophic.

Chapter 24
And so it Begins…

The army designated to go with Jen armed themselves with weapons and moved into formation. Micol and Jen led the way as they convened on the southernmost end of the field, while John remained closer to the temple courts with the units of men that Jared would lead. All of them were fully prepared for combat. It was there in that field that Jen prepared herself for what she was about to do. Micol wrapped the white linen cloth around her right arm and tied it. It would serve as her flag of surrender.

He looked at her with eyes of steel and unbending determination. "As soon as you open that portal, we will be right behind you. You will not be left alone and we will get Iyon back."

She closed her eyes and drew a deep breath in as she focused on only one thing; the river and everything it had just taught her. She looked at her friend and nodded her head. "I'll see you soon."

Jen turned from them and walked a short distance away. Letting herself go as she closed her eyes, Jen let the communication between the three of them begin. The first to speak was her father.

Jen, darling. My men and I are ready. As soon as you have trapped Tor and the troops have gone through, I will begin my mission to rescue your mother. Peace be with you, daughter. Know that I love you always.

And I you, Father.

An incredible force overtook them both, but more so with Jen as she prepared herself to take hold of something ungraspable.

The ancient power of the river combined its unfathomable strength with Jen's surrendered will. She raised her hand and formed a portal that led to the world where Iyon was last taken, to the very spot he had fallen. Jen walked through the portal but let it remain open behind her. With help from the strength of the Ancient, Jen reached out to Tor.

Tor, you vortex of abomination and terror; I am calling to you. It is me, Jen, and I wish to speak to only you! Come alone and I will surrender to you.

An eerie presence filled her mind as something unknown threaded its way into her thoughts. *How is it, Key Holder, that you are learning so fast the ways of the Ancient? And why would I come for you when Iyon has been destroyed? The army cannot continue for much longer without him. You all will fall and chaos and lawlessness will reign.*

Jen's hands formed fists as she clenched them to keep control.

You will come to me, for I know the secrets of who you are.

Impossible!

I know for I have read that your name is not Tor, but Lawless. That is what you truly are! Now come for me! For I am the great-great granddaughter of William John Hanning, who betrayed you and left you trapped and alone for years. Come alone and you can have your vengeance on me. I am at the exact spot where you took Iyon from me.

. . . .

By the time Jen had reached out to Tor, it was over half way done destroying the city of Eshron. While it was leveling beautiful stone buildings, it heard her calling to him. Surprised, it stayed completely still as Jen told the secret to Tor of who she really was. It looked around for Malum, but he had gone into the castle and was destroying it from the inside out. Tor vanished from the city, leaving Malum behind.

. . . .

The wind picked up and Jen stood her ground. She raised her hands in surrender, and hoped that it would not bind her hands in any way, for that would cause a problem for her. Appearing directly in front of Jen, Tor swirled around with its center black and furious. It looked like a horizontal tornado as it gazed upon the one it would seek vengeance on, although it was also suspicious of her surrender.

"Why would you willingly come to me, descendent of the one who betrayed me? Malum has plans to hand you over to Liel, but now that he has had his revenge, why should I not have mine? You must pay the price for the sins of your forefather and be imprisoned for many years. You will be kept in darkness as I was. Only when you are old and wrinkled will I hand you over to Liel."

"I will go with you, Lawless, and I will not fight your imprisonment. All I ask is to be taken to the one you took from me. Iyon was everything to me. When he was taken, I lost my reason to fight. So I have come to surrender so long as I can pay respects to the one that saved me."

"Well," the vortex said bluntly, "what is it to me that you say goodbye to a dead horse. I can see there are no others with you and there is no way in this universe you could overpower me. So, I will let you see him, but only for a few seconds. I need to finish destroying Eshron. I only have half the city leveled so far."

Ready yourself!

Jen remained in a catatonic state of surrender, acting as if she were accepting her fate. She felt both heat and inconceivable power as she had never experienced before surging through her veins. If it weren't for the power of the river giving her legs strength, she would have fallen flat to the ground under the incredible weight of it all. The surge ran through her arms as if they were on fire. With all this going on inside of her, Jen still managed to remain emotionless before the horrific anomaly that suspected nothing.

Jen put her head down and her hands were still in the air. "Agreed."

The vortex crept closer until the blackness was right up against her face.

"I have immeasurable power, human. So do not think you can run from me. Trick me in any way and I will make sure your days of imprisonment will be filled with pain and great misery. You cannot defeat me and who I am. I will also not allow you to transport all the way through to the other side. So, Jennifer Hanning; come and take your last step of freedom and enter into me."

Last step of freedom? So you think, Lawless!

"Do it, Lawless! Let me see my friend now." The portal that she held open behind her closed. "See, now I have no way to escape and you are so close to me I will have no time to create another and whisk myself away from your revenge. Let me say goodbye to Iyon."

The blackness swirled around like a whirlwind as slowly, a picture formed of Iyon lying lifeless on the Witch's altar. What happened next was done in a few seconds.

Jen stepped into the vortex. It was not like anything she had ever experienced in portal traveling. The wind whipped all around her. The sound was horrifying as if she were being run over by a hundred trains.

With her hands already in position, she reached out to the sides of the inner wall of the churning wind. Like an explosion, light energy burst out from Jen through her hands and the river of light intertwined with the swirling clouds of blackness. Before the vortex knew what had happened, the light energy coiled the entire inside of Tor. It screamed in terror as it knew it had been tricked and cursed Jen over and over. Jen looked behind her and nodded her head. Then turned and looked at the scene in front of her as the troops came running in. They ducked under her arms and entered into the Witch's lair. Lawless was powerless to stop them. Like venomous snakes they entered in with only this in mind; kill or be killed, and retrieve Iyon at any cost. ....

On the battlefield back in Tolare, John saw that Micol's army was moving forward through the portal. A smile crept across his face, as that meant his daughter's plan had worked. Now it was his turn!

John raised both hands to the air to form two portals. He felt fire and heat rage through him as pictures of the worlds of Earth flashed through his mind until he zeroed in on one; Free Earth, now Liel's Earth. The power of the Chest consumed John as he saw the dark planet in his mind and entered into it. When the underground gates that led to the lair appeared in his mind, the first portal was created for Jared and three units of men armed to the max. Their sole purpose was to create chaos and destruction wherever they went to divert the forces. The passageway led straight to the perimeter of Liel's underground castle. They were to attack it head-on.

The power for the second portal flowed through John's other hand, creating an entrance that led into a hallway somewhere deep inside the castle. From that point, he could only hope to find his way to her.

After John's work was completed, there were two swirling masses in the valley by the temple; one much larger in size than the other so that five lines of men could charge through at once.

Jared raised his fist in the air and in unison, the army roared a battle cry and ran as one, disappearing into the swirling mysterious power. Their mission was simple; to be heard, to fight and to the kill the Skeign with their weapons.

John and his men were to leave next. General Stantyon stood by John's side and together they walked into the portal. The few men that followed each held the most powerful guns in Tolare. Their mission was not as simple; not to be heard or seen, until it was too late for their enemies.

. . . .

Micol and his troops entered from the back of the cave entrance. They too, entered quietly and appeared right out of thin air. All the witches were found on their knees with their heads bent down to the ground and their hands folded behind their heads. The men wasted no time separating and moving like deadly vipers along the walls.

They mercilessly attacked the witches. Many were vaporized in a second. Others got up when they were pulled out of their collective trance by the Mother Witch. At least forty witches rose to their feet and began speaking dark and deadly incantations toward the troops. Some of Micol's men dropped to the ground as the spells cast on them sucked the life from their veins. Micol's heart pounded as he saw them fall lifeless.

"Kill them fast, men, or we will not walk out to see the light of day again!"

During the attack, the Witch Mother grabbed the glowing orb of blue waves and dashed into a side tunnel. Micol saw her leave and sought to make chase after her, but there were at least twenty witches in his path. With a gun in one hand and a sword that was coated with Iyon's own power and energy in the other, Micol jumped into the pool of witches. Every shot was a fatal kill and the sword slashed through two or three witches at a time, extinguishing their existence forever. He moved like lightning with perfect precision. There was nothing in that room that was faster than him.

A group of witches formed an orb of black fury in the air and cast it toward Micol, hoping to entrap his soul within it. But it was not to be. With innate and unexplainable instincts Micol flipped through the air, blasting the black orb with a Taser. He spun and landed, letting his blade slash through the group of witches who had created it. As soon as the blade ripped through them, they turned into black dust and were no more. During that same moment, others spewed death spells and curses into the air, directed toward Micol but saw that nothing happened to him, and that is when they realized who he was.

Fear filled their immoral bodies as they recognized the one they were fighting against.

"No! It couldn't be," said a few of the witches in unison. "Run, sisters, run! He has returned and will kill us all!"

As fate would have it, the son of the Captain had unknowingly found his way to them. The witches had lived all these years privately gloating in their secret capture of the great Captain Shan. But now it was as if the spirit of Shan was back and would have his revenge through the one that was his son. They gave in to their fear and ran away from Micol and the troops who were armed with weapons they no longer felt they could defeat.

The soldiers pursued them through the tunnels and one by one the witches were picked off and killed. After Micol had slain the group of witches and saw that his troops had the others on the run, he ducked into the tunnel in search of the Mother, all the while, not knowing that she was the one responsible for forming the plan that had killed his father.

. . . .

Jared's men formed four rows of fifty across and moved into fighting position. The first row knelt to one knee with the second row standing directly behind them while the third and fourth row remained back waiting in great anticipation before the entrance to the giant black castle that led into Liel's underworld lair.

Liel felt them enter his domain and went to stand by the pillar far above the castle gates. He gazed down at the men before him and scoffed and laughed. He was really quite amused by the bold and senseless attack being considered against him.

Jared wasted no time in challenging the one who the Skeign called 'Master.'

"We are the remnant of the free land, Liel, and we come against you! Send out your best so that we may destroy them this day!"

Liel shook his head and smiled pathetically at this ridiculous and entertaining charade.

"All right then; you think you can come against me? I will show you what I do to little mice like you!" Liel turned to his Skeign servant that was standing to the right of him, "Open the gates and send them out."

The servant bowed his head to the ground and scurried away. Liel gazed down at the humans before him. What gall they had to come to him. "Well, less to deal with later, I guess," he murmured to himself with a smile on his face.

The sound of a massive horn blew, vibrating the underworld, and the black iron gates of Liel's castle began to open. The pounding of the paws of the many Skeign creatures shook the rocks as they marched out to devour their prey as though they would be nothing more than a midday snack.

"Ready your weapons!" Jared commanded.

Every gun was raised and pointed at the oncoming mass of monsters headed straight their way. Jared kept a straight face, but celebrated on the inside. This would be the first time that weapons fashioned by the power of Iyon had ever been used. It would catch this army off guard. Finally, they would have their chance to show the enemy what it is like to be humiliated and suffer defeat.

. . . .

The caves became dark as the torches weakly fought to light the darkness. Micol chased the witch down to the darkest domains of the abyss where no man should dare to go. She made it to a chamber door that was lined with golden snake images. She looked behind her and saw Micol running down the hallway toward her. She scuffed and scowled in disgust and looked at the snakes.

"Wake up," she hissed, "Wake up from your slumber and kill him! Kill him!"

The bodies of the golden snakes came to life and within seconds, fell from the door and scurried toward the one they were ordered to kill.

Micol saw the witch disappear through the door. The poisonous snakes were now headed straight for him. He did not need to make a choice whether to run or stay and fight. It was not in him to run away. With a gun in one hand and a blade that glowed like blue fury in the other, Micol charged the snakes with one objective: kill them all and not be bitten.

If any had witnessed the next passing seconds, they would have recorded them as a superhuman feat. Micol twirled, ducked, bounced off walls and severed dozens of heads at once from the bodies of the snakes while blasting other heads off with his gun. In a matter of seconds, he was standing in a pool of lifeless, convulsing bodies that were oozing their green venomous blood over the dirt covered floor.

With an undeterred vengeance in his eyes, he moved on in pursuit of the witch. He opened the door and entered into her chamber.

. . . .

Lawless fought Jen with every passing second but to no avail. It tried to twist and move but she, with the power of the river flowing through her, held it fast. It was helpless against her will. And then it gave up the fight and solicited a solemn promise.

"You will pay for this; you and all your kind, unless you let me go."

"Not a chance." Jen stood fast with her arms in the air directly in the middle of the vortex. The river of white light continued to flow through her and out into the torrent of hatred and anarchy known as Lawless. Tears streamed down her face as her eyes remained steadfast on the lifeless body of Iyon on the other side of the witches' sanctuary. He had become a trustworthy friend; one that she could always rely on when she was weak.

Come back to me. Please, come back to me!

The vortex continued to fight her as she continued to wait on the soldiers' return.

....

Hundreds; no, thousands of Skeign marched toward the small band of fearless men with Jared. The gates behind them closed and the Skeign army came to a halt while they waited for the command of their Master.

The men steadied their weapons and waited. In Jared's mind, the clock was ticking. They would hold them off for only a few precious moments, in hopes that would be all that John would need to find his wife. With the invisible portal behind them to back right into, Jared knew they would make their escape with ease. He looked up and saw Liel by the pillar behind the castle walls. He was staring directly at him. Jared could feel his presence come over him and the men. Normally, they would've fallen under the depression by now, but Liel's presence was not what he expected it to be. He had been weakened. The plan was working.

Jared smiled victoriously and locked eyes with Liel, waiting for him to make his next move.

....

Adriana! It's me, John and I'm coming for you now. Where are you, my darling?

I was in my room, but I left a bit ago. The halls are empty. There is no one out right now. And I told you not to come.

Go to the red door, my dear and I will meet you there. Now go and hurry!

As Adriana walked down the silent hallway, her heart began to pump as if trying to push life back into her. Could he really have come for her? Finally, after all this time, maybe she would get a chance to at least see him.

Adriana picked up her teal-colored satin gown and began running down the hall. It would not be much longer until she would reach the door.

While all the Skeign were preoccupied with the offensive attack led by Jared and his men, John and his small band of men crept through the tunnels of the lower region of the castle unnoticed. The emerald rings that had been fashioned by Hope and given to all men and women that went on the mission shielded them well. They made their way to the lowest hall of the castle. The floor was made of smooth marble and the pillars were golden and decorated with intricate designs. The band of men looked around with an awful feeling in their gut as to what they just walked into. There on the other end of the hall was the red door that had no handle.

Can you see the door yet? John asked.

Yes! I am running to it.

His heart leapt in his chest and he started to run himself. The others called out to him but he did not hear them or care to. He just wanted to get to that door. General Stantyon cursed at the ground and waved the others to run after John. If they were running straight into an ambush, then they would not want to be cut off from John.

John waved at the men with his free hand not holding the gun. When he was between twenty and thirty feet from the door he stopped.

Stand on the side, Adriana and stay at a safe distance while we blast the door.

John looked behind him with a rushed panic on his face.

"Come on, hurry! We haven't much time before Liel will notice our presence here! Line up now. Aim your weapons….ready….fire!!"

. . . .

"Your men will die today, Jared, son of the Captain. But you will be taken as prisoner."

Liel raised his hands into the air. "Servants that are mine, ATTACK!"

The Skeign leaped and bounded to their unexpected and imminent death.

"Ready….FIRE!" commanded Jared.

Liel weakened and fell against the ledge in the tower. The guns being fired filled his kingdom with a power he did not see coming. The Skeign were vaporized, one after the other, without a chance to fight back. The weakness of his kingdom had brought the Master down to almost a human level, and only then did he realize that he had been tricked. John was in his kingdom and he had come for Adriana. A smile cringed across his face.

"Foolish man. Your heart is your weakness. It will be your undoing."

Liel pulled himself to his feet and stomped away from the battle. He ordered the remaining Skeign to fall back as the castle gates opened back up. Like ants retreating back to their den of safety, the Skeign fled behind its doors. There they would be protected from the deadly force carried along by the silent waves of power filled with blue thunder and electricity. By the time they had retreated, nearly a thousand of them had fallen.

Jared did not want to wait and gave the order, "Fall back!"

He knew the retreat only meant one thing. They were going after John.

Jared remained at the invisible portal entrance while the men fled into it.

He stared at the Skeign as they disappeared behind the gate, watching as it closed. Once Liel knew that John had infiltrated his realm, he reordered all his forces to pursue John. His action sent shivers down Jared's back. "You better hurry, my friend. I have given you all the time that I could."

As soon as every last man was safely through, Jared ducked into the portal and was gone from that world.

Chapter 25
Death and Sacrifice

John's body shook with anger and frustration. The blasting of the door had little to no impact. He thought for sure the weapons they now had would have done the job. But he kept his aim against the door with no intention of stopping for any reason; that is, until General Stantyon gently placed his hand on John's shoulder.

"John, stop. It's not working. We're going to have to find another way. We only had minutes to do this and that time is up. We have to go now."

Whether it was the anger that caused his tears or the desperation at having been so close to rescuing Adriana made no difference to John; he let the gun fall to his side in shameful defeat. And the ground began to shake from the pounding of a thousand Skeign rushing toward them.

"John, make the portal now. We will fight another day. Let's go." The General's anxious tone reverberated through John's ears. He understood the order, but he did not want to leave his wife behind again.

The Skeign stormed the hall straight toward them. With only seconds left, John raised his hand and the portal was created. Immediately the men fled in until all that remained were the General and John. John had no intention of going back and that's when General Stantyon made his move. He moved swiftly behind John and twisted his free arm behind his back and thrust him through the portal. Liel had entered the hall and caught sight of John before he disappeared into the portal and sent him a message that others could not hear.

I see you now, John! The men with the burning red chains will be visiting your wife soon. She will burn but I will see to it that she will not die. I am weary of this game with you and so now it ends. You have one hour to surrender before her torment begins. Do not think I am, as you humans say, bluffing. This will happen to her. You have sixty minutes, John!

The portal closed with the team safely on the other side back in the field before the temple and its courtyard. General Stantyon held John tight until a few soldiers removed the weapon from his hand. Only then did he let go of John, who angrily jerked himself away, giving the General a look of betrayal.

"My orders were to ensure that if the mission failed, that you would make it back to us. We can't fight this battle without you, John. I'm sorry we didn't succeed, but we will find a way. You forget, I know you. You would've stayed, but we can't allow that. Tolare needs you."

There's not enough time for another plan! I am out of time.

"You okay now?" General Stantyon asked.

John only stared blankly at him. The General looked at the others who were about to apprehend John for his own safety when John raised his hands in surrender. Jared rushed over to see if Adriana was with them and saw the scuffle taking place between John and General Stantyon.

"Yeah, I'm good. I'm in shock; so can you just give me a few minutes alone, please?" John pleaded.

The General didn't like the way John was acting and didn't want him left alone. He hated having to treat John like this, but for the man's own safety, he had no choice.

"We need to report to Hope, and then you can be alone if she allows." The others circled him at close proximity. "No offense, John, but I know how hard this is for you. No sudden moves now. The last thing I want to do is embarrass you here. Let's just go."

The General looked at Jared. "This is a quiet take-in, Jared. I know what is going through this man's head right now and we can't let him do it."

Jared moved to one side of John while Taq took the other. John dropped his head in defeat. He did not want to fight his own comrades and his friends. They each gently grabbed John by the elbow, knowing to apply forceful pressure if they had to. With every step, John could not stop thinking about an escape. He would only need a couple seconds, but General Stantyon knew this also, and was not about to give him that kind of freedom.

They reached the center of the temple court and stood on the platform, waiting for it to turn as it always did before lowering into the great abyss. With every passing micro-second, John felt the hopelessness envelop his soul. He knew that this time, Hope would keep him apprehended for his own safety. There was no talking his way out of it.

The platform began to turn…

. . . .

Micol let the door slam behind him. Finally, the Witch Mother had no place to run. She was cornered and faced the one she would have no choice but to kill or be killed herself. The room was barren, except for two pedestals. An orb rested on each. One was glowing brighter than the sun and was mixed with blue waves, along with thunder and lightning. The other was covered with a layer of black hardened tar. The witch was standing between the two. With her hands raised, she recited an incantation and created a black cloud filled with deadly poisons that could kill a man's soul in a single breath. Her thick pasty skin pulsated with evil as she stared hungrily at the boy. Then, she laughed.

"It is fate that you, the son of the Captain of the worlds of Earth, would find your way to me, just as your father did, so long ago."

Micol faltered a step at the mention of his father. Years of pent up anger, rage and the desire for revenge exploded inside him. These were emotions that fed the very root of evil. The Mother saw her opportunity and she took it. She raised her hand toward the boy as if she was choking him and immediately, his body was thrust up against the door and he gasped for air. She was choking the life out of him.

"Oh, foolish boy; this is going to be easier than I thought. How do you think your father died? On his missions of surveying the cities, you think? The presence of both your father and the Warrior General disappeared, did it not? So that wretched Hope thought they were dead."

The witch jerked her hand. Micol's body burst through the air and slammed against the opposite wall, his throat constricted by the Mother's witchcraft. Feeling like she was overtaking him, she inched her way closer to him. "It was I and my children, Micol, who captured them. Yes! It was a glorious trap, indeed. And when we were done with them, we directed the mountains to fall on them, crushing their bodies," she finished with a smile. Her countenance changed as she looked at Micol and said, "And now it's time to kill you."

The Witch Mother reached back toward the black cloud of death, and thrust her hand forward; causing the black cloud to fly toward Micol and completely surround him. She released her death grip so that Micol would have no choice but to breathe in the deadly fumes that the witch had created. He fell to the ground; his body was engulfed in the black cloud as it swirled erratically around him. He could hear the witch laugh sadistically.

As Micol gasped for breath, he waited for death to take its grip upon his soul. Nothing happened. He took another cautious breath. Again, nothing happened. Micol stood to his feet and readied his sword. Although he was still encased inside the cloud of death, he saw exactly where she was standing, still laughing away. Micol used the back wall and propelled himself out of the cloud of death. He aimed the sword for the heart of the witch.

Her laugher paused as she gazed for one second at the impossible taking place, and then in another second, the sword was thrust through her heart. Her body broke apart before Micol and turned into a small black pile of ashes. The Mother Witch was no more. And with her death, all her remaining children dropped dead as the powerful witchcraft that held their life was now destroyed. Every last one of them broke apart and turned into ashes. Triumphantly, Micol walked over to the glowing blue orb, removed it, and started his journey back to the sanctuary.

. . . .

And that's when it hit John. They would be traveling downward on the platform. His hand was already pointed down. It was all too easy and no one would get hurt. John's close friends and comrades made the mistake of letting go of the grip they had on him now that they were seconds from Hope. As the platform lowered, he motioned his hand and created a very small portal directly below him; so as they dropped into the abyss, John simply vanished from them. The portal closed immediately, leaving the men looking in great dismay at one another. They looked to Hope for what could be done for John. She remained silent as her light waves of deep yellow and dark orange illuminated the room.

"There was no stopping him. Leave us, for now. Go back to the camp; tell no one that John is gone from us. Let the armies return to their campground and continue their training and forging of weapons. They will all be needed when the time comes."

Jared, stricken with tears, spoke up, "Hope, what will become of John?"

"Leave that to us."

The men headed back to the camp, all of them, paled with shock at what John had decided to do.

. . . .

Jen almost leapt from the vortex when she saw Micol emerge, carrying a glowing orb in his hands. Feeling confident that the vortex would cause no more problems, Jen stepped out of it. She knew that it would not be needed any further. The waves of light retracted from the whirling mass of destruction.

"Cause us trouble today, Lawless, and I will entrap you again. You may think you are powerful, but you forget that the force of light is always and will forever be stronger than the force of darkness. Now go!" Jen spoke confidently as the vortex, ashamed of its weakness, vanished from their sight.

With a smile ear to ear, she ran to Micol and wrapped her arms around him. He laughed. "Hey now, careful here. I think I'm holding Iyon in my hands." Jen turned and placed her hand on the glowing orb and felt its warm heat. Immediately, his presence filled her being. She could sense him, though he could not speak to her. Jen took the orb from Micol's hands and walked over to Iyon's lifeless body. She wasn't sure what to do, so she closed her eyes and let her instincts take over. The orb floated out of Jen's hands and connected with the gem upon the golden breastplate. As soon as the two touched, the entire orb absorbed into the gem until it disappeared. Jen backed away from the body as a powerful force filled the Warrior Horse. Iyon breathed in and out several times, each time more powerful than the next until he opened his eyes and stood to his feet. Jen wrapped her arms around his neck as he bent his head down until it was pressing against her back.

"Now you have come back for me. Thank you, my friend."

The soldiers, having returned from different parts of the cave after all the witches had died, stood in silent pride and gratitude as they saw the two together again. For that moment, a small victory had been won, and tears of joy were shed.

Iyon raised his head and peered down the tunnel that led to the Witch Mother's domain. "Come with me now. There is something I must show you."

Micol motioned to his men and said to Jen, "We'll be waiting here and standing watch. Whatever it is you need to do, please do it quickly. We do need to get back and see how your father's mission progressed."

Jen nodded and disappeared into the dark tunnels following Iyon.

Chapter 26
Taken

John landed by the red door, where he had last disappeared from Liel's sight. Liel and his Skeign were waiting for him. Bravely, John pulled himself to his feet and faced Liel.

"Impressive, John; you moved more quickly than I thought you could."

"I did. Now hold up your end of the agreement, Liel."

"Alright; I will leave her alone, for now. You and your cursed daughter have been thorns in my side for long enough. Causing me trouble comes with a cost, John. I will see to it that your wife will be my servant forever. She will be the one to help me defeat your daughter for I know that her training has barely started. She will be as easily manipulated as you were. And then Tolare will fall, John. And everyone there will be slain."

"You're a fool, Liel! For one who deceives and manipulates, you have no clue how blind you are! You will not win this war. You are the one that is condemned."

Liel pointed his finger at John, causing the sensation of a thousand knives stabbing across John's body as he fought to breathe, but nothing would enter his lungs. Liel smiled at him as his body convulsed and he almost died right there. Liel released him, causing John to collapse to the ground before him.

"It disgusts me, how pathetically weak you humans are. Your entire race is a disease that needs to be purged."

"Why don't you just kill me now?" John gasped as he struggled to his feet. The Skeign servants behind him used their tail-like tentacles and grabbed hold of John, forcing him to his feet faster to face their Master.

"Because I cannot deprive my army the celebration of your capture. Your public mocking will be a great entertainment for my servants. It will strengthen them to see you suffer." Liel turned his attention to the servants holding John up, "I'm done with him. Take him to the stadium now and bind him to the whipping post." Watching him being dragged off, Liel thought of yet a more pleasing punishment. "Wait! Bring him back to me." The Skeign servants dragged John back to face Liel.

"Do you think my enemy is more powerful than I? I can tell you that my plan is divine and perfect. Mankind will not prevail over my onslaught of them." Liel smiled devilishly and held out his own hands in front of him. His hands turned black and formed a set of heavy handcuffs that looked like smoldering tar and reeked of rotting flesh and death.

John's hands were uncontrollably jerked in front of him by Liel just thinking it. He grabbed John by his forearms, held them tight as the cuffs floated in the air and forcibly attached around John's wrists. Immediately they bonded to his skin as if they were now a part of him, while sending a virulent poison into his bloodstream.

John did his best to hold his tongue, but he could not resist for the poison felt like a wild fire spreading throughout his body.

Liel, confident of his powers, stepped away from John and held his hands out. "Go ahead, John, try to create your precious portal now so that you can escape from me. If you can still manage to make one, I will let you and your wife go. I give you my word."

John held up his hand and with everything within him, he tried, but the poison in his blood was too strong. He tried again and again, and still he failed.

Liel laughed at him, and the Skeign creatures grunted in fiendish delight at John's pathetic attempts to do as Liel said.

"Come on, John! Perhaps you're not trying hard enough! Are you weak? Is the river I know you have bonded with not more powerful than I? Try!

Try harder!" Liel was yelling in delight until John fell to his knees in exhaustion. Liel walked toward him and bent right over him so that he could whisper near John's ears. "You see, John, I can't be beat. My power is strong. This is what will happen to your kind, you human garbage."

Liel straightened so he could tower over his fallen prey. "Now you may take him to the stadium. Have your fun with him, but do not kill him. I still have plans for him."

They dragged John to the entrance of a great stadium. And there, men dressed head to toe in black robes ripped his shirt off. John could hear the resounding cheers and roars of those that filled the stadium. It sounded like a mixture of both men and beasts. With his hands forever chained, he was shoved through the chamber doors that led into the stadium and the men in robes dragged him to the center. They threw him to the ground. Surrounding the arena was a stadium filled with cheering Skeign and to John's horrific surprise, men and woman sat among them, all eager to witness his beating.

One of the iron gates in the arena opened and a Skeign creature emerged, its tail of tentacles full of strands of metal cords. Each contained electric pulses flowing through them. The next Skeign in charge of this public humiliation came out and gleefully danced around John while the other periodically whipped him with a single strand, sending electricity through John's body. The convulsing of John's body caused the crowd to cheer wildly. They roared and drooled in delight. As John tried to run from the beast, it mocked him and tripped him with metal-like tentacles.

Other Skeign creatures entered into the stadium and had their fun with John. They tossed him back and forth from one to another, catching him and shocking him. They continued on with other cruel games meant for humiliation and mockery for what seemed like hours until a bell sounded. The time of mocking was finally over.

Liel gave the order that after the public mocking, John's feet were to be bound in front of all the Skeign; he was gagged with a metallic wrap secured tightly around his head. They attached a chain to his feet and dragged him to the gate that led out of the arena. The crowd roared in great delight. He was taken all the way to the great red door. Only Liel had the power to open this door and enter through. Liel was standing in front of the red door, waiting for his prisoner to be brought to him; a trail of John's blood was left behind as his back had been cut and bloodied. Once the chain was brought to him, Liel jealously grabbed it and told his servants to leave. Soon, he was alone with just John.

"Clever of you to figure out that your wife was behind these doors. However, it was stupid of you to think that you could ever breach them on your own. Only I can open these doors, fool. Your dear wife will be right down the hall from you. Pity she will never know that you are here as well."

Liel placed his left hand on the door and it began to glow like fire. The energy that came from the beast-like man surged through the doors and slowly they opened. Liel dragged John in and the door shut behind them.

They entered a hall. Luxuriously elegant, the floors were made of marble. The pillars that lined the hall were layered with precious, glistening gemstones, filling the halls with a rainbow of color. John was perplexed that deep in Liel's lair was an area full of a warmth and comfort Liel so deviously portrayed. Liel looked behind him and smiled down at John, but his smile vanished and he stopped abruptly. "Oh no, we simply can't have that here in these halls."

Liel snapped his fingers and slaves ran to him and threw themselves at his feet, putting their faces all the way to the ground before him.

"Clean this blood up! There can be no trace of foul play in these halls." The slaves jumped into action, cleaning up the mess as Liel proceeded down the hall until he came to a door, laced with gold and jewels. The number on the door was 227.

"You see now, John. I am taking good care of your wife. I'm glad you thought of the need to save her. It was our plan all along. She is living better now than what you could ever provide for her. I'd let you say hi, but all my subjects have been put into a deep sleep right now. Wouldn't want any of them seeing you like this, now would I? They'll get theirs when I'm done with them."

He laughed manically as he yanked at the chain. "Moving on!" John gazed at the door as long as he could. How badly he wanted to call out to her, hold her in his arms one more time, but that was exactly what had gotten him here and now there was no way he would ever be any help to Hope, Iyon, Tolare, or his beloved daughter. As long as Liel had Adriana, John knew that surrender was his only option. Still, an incredible sense of failure filled his soul as Liel pulled him into another hallway sealed by closed doors made of a dark metal.

"You see these doors, John? They never open while my servants are out of their rooms and doing my daily bidding for me. Oh if some of them only knew the torture that goes on down these halls!" Liel laughed again. John's heart sank further.

They entered through those doors and John fought hard to stay conscious. The amount of pain ringing throughout his body caused him to lose track of time as Liel pulled him along. Liel entered through another secured door that revealed yet another hallway. The floor of this hallway was coarse and scraped John's back as he was dragged along. He looked to his left and his right while he desperately tried to lift his back away from the coarse ground. On both sides of the hall were sealed doors. They were black and contained no handles or knobs of any kind. Guards stood in front of the last door. This doorway was not like the others. It was a double doorway entrance. The guards were not typical Skeign creatures, but dragons instead. John looked up and to his surprise; each dragon had a chain around its neck and they were both chained directly to the doors. As Liel approached, the dragons bowed their heads to the ground.

"My slaves," he called out to them in a very triumphant tone, "you have been chained to these doors for many seasons with no one to guard. This day, I am giving you a Key Holder. You are to guard him with your lives until the day comes when I have need of him again. If anyone but me ever comes here, you will attack and kill no matter what or who it is. No one besides me is ever to pass through the doors that you are eternally bound to.

"Yes, Master," they spoke in unison as their heads bowed to the ground.

"Now, open the doors!" Liel commanded them.

In unison, the dragons strained against their chains as they struggled to open the doors leading to the prison room. Each door was at least two feet thick.

Once the doors opened, Liel dragged John in behind him. The room had a peculiar oval shape to it. The center featured a raised cylinder made out of concrete with a small metal bar at the base of it. This raised base was no more than a foot high and just a few feet in diameter. Two humans were in front of the cylinder, bowing low to the ground. They wore black robes and metal masks, their faces completely covered. They were two men that surrendered to the will of Liel long ago and were now solely faithful to him.

Liel threw the chain toward them. "Get up you buffoons! Prepare the Key Holder for hibernation." The humans sprung to their feet, not daring to look up at the Master. They grabbed John and took him to the center of the room and secured his chain to the raised bar on the small circular platform. They took a thick leather strap and wrapped it around John's upper torso, securing his arms tightly against his body. His fears kicked in and he fought against the chains and strap, knowing full well that it was in vain, and in seconds, he would be rendered useless. If there was a way to have a plan, now was the time. Surely, there could have been another way to rescue Adriana, if she had even wanted rescuing.

Once John was secure, the men in robes went to the wall and pulled down a lever. John floated straight up, and would've continued if it weren't for being chained to the bar.

"Time to sleep, John, but this form of sleep you're not going to like. You thought the chamber you were trapped in before was bad. I lost Dangor because of you and your daughter, and he was very effective at his job. In time, you will reveal those secrets to me if I cannot retrieve Dangor. But for now, you will simply be out of my way. One Key Holder down and one to go! Oh and John, you will be seeing me in your dreams."

Liel walked to the opposite wall and pulled down a second lever. The base of the cylinder lit up with a glowing red color. The glow transported over to John and traveled up and over John's body, encasing him until the glow connected with the cylinder shaped base on the ceiling above. John was thrown into unconsciousness and remained floating in the air.

Liel looked at the captured Key Holder and proudly admired his handiwork. With a smirk, he victoriously left the room. The dragons shut the doors by backing into them until both doors were secure, locking the Key Holder up, until he would be needed again. For now, that was the end of John William Hanning.

Chapter 27
A Dawn of Hope

Iyon and Jen traversed the dark tunnels until they approached the room where Micol had killed the Mother Witch. Against the barren wall were the two pedestals; one was now empty. The other held an orb that was covered in the thick black tar which over the years had hardened and molded itself to the pedestal.

The gem embedded in Iyon's breastplate glowed with great intensity and then like a rainbow prism, the light waves moved out from it and traveled to the tar-covered orb. Gently and carefully, the colors of light went to work against the hardened tar as if massaging it. The tar began to loosen its hold and flake off like black snowflakes floating to the floor. When the surgery was complete, the rainbow of light departed from it and returned back into the gem upon Iyon's breastplate. They gazed at a new, brightly glowing orb and within it appeared ocean waves. The room filled with a powerful presence. Jen and Iyon were incased in heat waves and felt the trapped soul within the orb pleading for escape.

"Jen," Iyon quietly spoke as his eyes glistened with the colors of the sea. "I'd like you to meet the real Malum."

Awestruck, a shiver ran down her back at the incredible discovery that meant one truly great thing, Iyon was not the last Warrior after all.

"How did you know, Iyon?"

"When she placed me in here, I could still see the outside world. When

I looked over and saw the orb plastered in black tar on the pedestal, I just knew. I knew it was him. I still don't know who he is or how this is possible; he is a Warrior Horse that was never known by Hope or my father. But yet, here lies his soul, and he is wondrously strong. We must find Malum now; but how we can find him, I have no clue."

A smile lit up Jen's face. "I know exactly where he is. Eshron — right where the vortex deserted him."

"Then we haven't a moment to lose. Get the orb and I'll take you back to the others."

Excitement filled her heart as Jen lifted the orb from its prison and held it carefully in her hands. Iyon kneeled so she could easily climb up and straddle him.

In moments, they met up with Micol and his men. When they shared what they had learned — that there could once again be two Warrior Horses among them — the small crowd reveled with happiness. The decision was made; they would venture straight to Eshron. But to be safe, Jen created two portals, one leading home for Micol's men to go through and the other was to Eshron. Only a small group would be needed for this mission. As soon as the men disappeared into the portal that led to Tolare, Micol, Jen and Iyon disappeared into the one that led to Eshron.

· · · · · · · · · · · ·

Smoke and dust filled the air. The three of them stood and stared in disgust, remembering the city that once was. But now, half of it was demolished. There was not even a hint of the buildings that once were.

"Unbelievable," commented Micol. "It's like they wanted to erase it from ever having existed."

"Let's find Malum, he's probably in the castle."

Iyon cut her off, "What castle?"

As the dust and smoke cleared, they looked for the magnificent castle that had stood the test of time for so many generations, but it was no more. Emerging out of the smoke of destruction came the dark horse. He pounded his hooves and his eyes flared a deadly crimson red as he stared again at his arch enemy.

"Iyon! How can this be? When I left, you were dead. You are supposed to be my servant! How is it that the witches have failed in this…" Malum stopped short as his eyes drifted to the orb in Jen's hands, no longer covered in tar. His ears pricked back.

"I see," he said, low and monotonic. "You wish to free him, don't you? Not going to happen, Iyon! This body belongs to me now!" He flicked a nervous glance around, noticing that Tor was nowhere to be seen.

"It won't be coming to your aid today, Malum." Jen spoke out. "I dealt with Tor, and now…we're going to deal with you."

Each move to one side while I hit him head-on. We have to pin him.

Jen looked at Micol, who had his weapon already drawn; she signed a v-shape behind her back. He nodded, understanding her. The three launched their attack.

Malum reared up as Iyon bolted toward him. Micol aimed his weapon for the two back legs and shot at Malum. His aim was true as the bolt of power and energy knocked out the horse's knees. Then Iyon made his move. He let the power surge through his eyes. Both power and energy came from the force within Iyon; power strong enough to move mountains from their positions and oceans from their boundaries. He let the power surge into Malum's eyes and this time, it sunk deep inside him. Malum roared like a dragon as the pain from the light attacked his dark and evil soul. Malum crashed to the ground, unable to move. Iyon kept his aim true and did not withdraw the force. Jen ran in with the glowing orb and wasted no time. She thrust it into the chest of the frantic beast and jumped away. Iyon released the animal and let the power within the orb do the rest.

Malum struggled to his feet but was thrown back down. "Nooo! Get off me. Get off me. You will never win this battle. The coming days of darkness cannot be stopped. You fools! You ignorant fools!"

An explosion of light enveloped Malum as the orb broke, letting the life force that had been trapped for so many years back into the body it once had inhabited. The fight did not last long, for there was nothing the darkness inside the beast could do. As light filled Malum, a thick black cloud came off him. In one last cry; the evil that filled this Warrior's body had to release its prisoner. The cloud rose into the air and the wind carried it away.

Afterward, lying on the ground was the authentic Malum. His body was purified and as white as the first winter's snowfall glistening against the light of the sun. He raised his head, shook it and looked over to the three who had saved him, but his eyes fell last on Iyon. He got to his feet and walked a few paces toward them and nodded in admiration and deep gratitude.

He then looked up at Iyon and the two stared at one another. The eyes of the two Warriors were identical, and that was an impossible truth. Malum revealed the revelation.

"Our father would be most proud of you, my brother."

Iyon took a step back but did not take his eyes off Malum. The possibility of the General of all Warrior Horses having more than one heir was always considered unfathomable. A Warrior Horse can only reproduce once in their lifetime. Under no circumstance could the General have ever had two, but yet; here they stood. It was an incredible anomaly, one that was good.

"And my name is not Malum, that was given to the black beast. Call me Dunamis, my brother, for that is the name Father called out as he perished. Long live Soterios."

"Long live Soterios," Iyon repeated. The name had not crossed his lips for a long time. The very name humbled him and his piercing blue eyes glistened with tears that came from the pit of his aching soul.

They both looked over to Jen. "Make the portal, Jen," Iyon humbly said. "It's time for us to go home."

And so it was out of the ashes of Eshron that a new Warrior was reborn. Though the road ahead would not be an easy one, at least now, it was more enlightened than it had been for many years.

Chapter 28
Unwanted News and Secrets Revealed

Jen thought it was only fitting that their triumphant entry be made right in the heart of the city. As soon as eyes laid on them, it was like the heart of the city stopped beating. Whispers of quiet excitement swept through the crowds and then one townsman, no longer able to hold in his excitement, hollered to all who could hear him, "Ring the bells! Ring the bells! Look now, Iyon is no longer alone. There are now two Warriors among us. There are two!"

The city people burst out cheering. Word spread for the bells to be rung as the crowd pressed in to gaze on what their eyes had so longed to see.

Micol climbed onto Dunamis and Jen onto Iyon so that they would not get lost in the crowd.

They marched in victory through the town until they hit the trail that led to the temple looming just up the hill from the city below. Jen had never felt so proud before. The mission that was expected to bring back the dead body of Iyon instead led to the miracle of his recovery and the discovery of his brother. Her mind raced at what they could do to defeat the enemy, and maybe even take back Tran, the beloved city that fell to Dolorous and ultimately, Liel. Jen could not wait to tell her father all the news. She was confident that his mission had succeeded also. Finally things were looking up.

As they entered the court, General Santyon, Jared, Fox and Taq greeted them. They knew Jen would be returning soon and so waited for her, knowing full well that she would need them for emotional support.

They gazed in wonder at the miracle before them at seeing two Warriors, but the distant look in their faces spoke a thousand words, and John was nowhere to be seen.

Jen looked to Fox for answers for her unsettling heart as she stared at their blank faces. "Where is my father, Fox?"

He looked up at her but could not find the right words to say.

Jen knew her father was gone. Her body caved in and her head fell on Iyon's neck as she clutched his mane, unable to breathe from the pain she felt in her heart. Her comrades and friends surrounded her as they tried to console her. They walked to the circular platform that would lower into the cavern where the floating tree containing the essence of Hope, resided. As they moved below the earth, Jen buried herself in Iyon's mane and sobbed horribly. Everyone waited in silence until Jen regained control. She slid off Iyon as Micol slid off Dunamis and came to stand by her side.

Hope cast light waves across the bottomless cavern. Jen let the waves hit her as one would let the waves of a gentle sea collide against their body. It entered her and soothed her pain. Soon, Jen regained her composure and waited for Hope to speak.

"Jen," Hope spoke softly. "There is no easy way to say what happened with your father's mission today. He and the group did return from the failed mission, but your father wanted to go back. His friends here tried to apprehend him in order to protect him from the fate that he chose willingly, but he cunningly escaped. He returned and surrendered himself to Liel. I'm sure he felt he had to in order to spare Adriana's life. I can tell you that Liel would not have killed him for he has need of him; but for now, we have no way of rescuing either of them. I am so sorry, Jen."

The words shredded her heart. He had left her again. Moments of dinner at the table, times of running with her dad, talks with her mom; they were just...gone, fallen into a pit of hopeless despair that seemed impossible to retrieve ever again. Jen turned toward Iyon and buried her head against his neck as he wrapped his neck around her. The visions of her old life faded into nothingness. She wiped her face and collected herself as two enormous truths set in. She now was truly the last Key Holder in this land, and there was nothing she could do to recover either of her parents.

"Well," Jen concluded with her newfound inner strength. "Then there is nothing else to do but win this war. I will do whatever I have to, Hope. And if Liel kills my parents, then I will do what I have to in this war to bring down his kingdom and make him pay for what he did, not just to me, but to all the others that have lost the ones they loved. I promise you, from this day forward, my life is dedicated to his demise." An unexplainable strength helped Jen to say these words. These days Jen had learned that her survival depended on relying on this newfound strength. Her understanding of what it was like to let this unfathomable energy surge through her for the days to come were imperative.

"Your father would be proud," Hope spoke tenderly, "and I could not be more pleased at the success of your mission. My own heart was strengthened as I sensed two Warriors entering Tolare. It is something I thought would never happen in our lifetime. I felt the strength of Soterios himself here as you entered. And do my eyes deceive me, or do I see two of his heirs standing before me?"

Now it was Dunamis' turn to speak. "Your eyes do not deceive you, great and ancient wonder, for through the witches' treachery of capturing our father's dying life force from within him, they did create me."

"Please, Malum," Hope cut him off, "you must tell us the mystery to the disappearance of the Captain and Soterios. Many years ago they were on some routine missions of mine; surveying cities, and then their life forces were both stolen. But we could never find any remains of them. Since then, there has been no closure for the army or the family."

Micol came to stand next to his brother for support. Jared put his arm around his younger brother, knowing that the next few minutes would bring both pain and relief at finally knowing what had become of their father.

"Let me begin by saying my true name is not Malum. Our father called out to me the name, Dunamis, giving me that name, because he knew I would need to be one of great strength in order to survive the captivity, and now I will tell you my story.

"That was the problem right there, Hope. They were on routine missions and the witches had tracked these routines. They knew exactly where they would be and at what time they would be there. So when they were in between cities, they were cleverly ambushed. I cannot tell you the specifics of how the witches managed to take down both the Captain and the General of Warriors. In my mind, they were not alone in this ambush. Someone else had to be involved. The truth of the matter is when they were taken to a realm of great mystery only known as the Witch's Abyss; they were cut off from you which meant you presumed them both dead. But they were still very much alive. The Captain was poisoned by the witches and was held captive by their many incantations while Soterios was chained to the poles upon their altar.

"It was a long and torturous process which lasted many months. For endless days, they surrounded him and cast spell after spell in an attempt to use their black magic to create a foal from his life source. After many failed attempts at procreating me, one day they finally succeeded. I was born white and pure as my father was. At that point, Soterios was depleted of his resources and was on his death bed. The first few days of my life, I would lie next to him, terrified of what my future would be. While I was still just a babe the witches took him from me. They placed him and Captain Shan at the bottom of a cavern somewhere in the realm of the Witch's Abyss. They cast a spell on the mountain and it collapsed on them. I wish I could say their days of captivity were without pain, but that would not be the truth.

"I was raised by them, but as a prisoner. When I was a little more grown but not powerful enough to fight them, they took me out of my prison, chained me to the same altar with those wretched poles they had chained my father to, and cast my soul into an orb. It was a tomb they fashioned to secure me while they used my body for their own evil purposes and gave that creature the name Malum. The body color turned black as death and it was their plan for him to grow in great strength and power. Yet there was a small part of him that hated what they did to him for he endured much pain through the process.

"I watched for days from the pedestal at the transformation of my body. The witches kept Malum chained until they had fully empowered him with their witchcraft. They eventually found out that I could still see out from within the orb, so they took even that away from me by pitching it with tar. They cast me away to a room where the Witch Mother practiced her incantations day after day."

Dunamis' voice lowered as he continued solemnly, "The creature that took over my body was enraged and full of spiteful revenge to know that my true brother was alive and well. He and the sons of the Captain were a great threat to them all. That is why Malum sought after all of you the way he did. He wanted all the heirs wiped out. But you have defeated them, and I thank you for freeing me from that prison of darkness. That is my story, Hope. That is truly how I came into being. What the witches meant for evil has been turned into good."

"Well then, son of Soterios, you should have what rightfully belongs to you. I never knew why I did what I did many seasons ago, but things have a way of coming full circle. This belongs to you," Hope spoke joyfully.

To the surprise of all, from out of the glowing light from within the tree floated a golden breastplate. It flew over Dunamis' neck and fastened onto him. The other half of the gem flowed out next. It was the gem that Hope had broken in two so long ago when it was first placed on the breastplate of Iyon. It floated to Dunamis and firmly fastened itself onto the front of the breastplate.

Dunamis bowed his head in humility as he was honored with this incredible gift. The two Warriors looked almost identical now, except for the fact that Dunamis was slightly more muscular than Iyon. But other than that, the brothers were the same.

"You have greatly honored me. Thank you," he humbly said.

"This is a great thing indeed. The people will have a renewed sense of hope and it was what we desperately needed. Let the people see both of you and there will be dancing in the streets once more. But for tonight, return to your places of rest and replenish your energy. Iyon, show your brother all of Tolare. Jen, return to Dahlia's this evening. Eat and rest. The days ahead are unknown and will be tumultuous, but our strength and hope will get us through this. There is much to be decided for the future that I must work out. Go for now and be at peace. What must be done will be done."

At that, the platform lifted and the small band of warriors soon stood in the outer temple courts. The Tolarian sun was setting in the west behind the trees of the forest.

Micol looked over at Jen, who was watching the sun as it disappeared.

"Jen, I'm going to head back to camp with my brother. Will you be ok?" he asked as he put his hand on her shoulder.

Jen looked at him, her heart broken, but knowing she had no choice but to stay strong. "I will be. I just need some time."

"Let us know if you need anything. We are all here for you."

She nodded her head. "Thanks Micol, for everything."

Micol went with General Stantyon, Taq, Fox and Jared, and they headed toward the field where the trail would wind its way through the forest and end at the army camp on the other side.

Iyon rubbed Jen's back as if trying to comfort her.

Come Jen, let me take you back to Dahlia's.

She straddled Iyon's back and in moments, they flew with Dunamis at Iyon's side and soon, they had arrived at Dahlia's.

After Dahlia met the brother of Iyon, they departed into the air and Jen was treated to Dahlia's amazing stew and comfort. Dahlia sat across from Jen as they ate together. Though she said nothing negative, Dahlia mourned the loss of John in her own quiet way. She looked out the window, put her elbow on the table and leaned her hand on her face, covering her mouth with her hand. "Oh that John," she spoke tenderly, then shook her head and laughed and cried all at once. "Always getting himself into trouble. This war…it's taken so many now. But there will be a light out of this, Jen. Sometimes you gotta fight a little longer, hold on a little tighter, and then when all seems lost and you just can't do it anymore, there it is; the light at the end of the storm. It comes, just like that, and it's all over."

The two cleaned their dinner bowls and as Jen retired to what had become both her and her father's room as the two never seemed to be there at the same time, Dahlia gently placed her hands on Jen's cheeks.

"Sweet Jen, stay strong and confident. You will see him again. Now take rest, child. You will need it for all the days to come."

"Yes, ma'am," Jen said in gratitude, "And thank you…for never giving up. It keeps me strong."

"Always and forever, my dear." She released Jen and retired to her own place of rest for the night.

As the stars filled the sky, Jen laid her head on the bed and found her place in the dream world. It was there that she so often found her family together; fighting against the forces that unceasingly tried to pull them apart, and so ended the night.

Chapter 29
The Pain of Betrayal

Adriana stared blankly into the mirror before her. Her hair hung in layers of unique perfection. A gentle mix of diamonds, rubies and emeralds glistened on her necklace and earrings. The satin deep green dress clung to her body just the way she had always wanted a dress to. She had everything she could dream of except the one thing she sacrificed, her family. She felt she had done the right thing, but the emptiness inside her told her otherwise.

The door opened and a male figure walked in. His elusive presence emanated throughout the room. One part of her wanted to run and the other part wanted to run to him. What was it about this being that so easily ensnared her?

He came up behind her as she stared in the mirror and rested his hands on her shoulders.

"Well done, Adriana. I never doubted for a second that you could lure him here."

A tear of betrayal ran down her cheek.

"So is it done?"

"As promised, he is safe and asleep, of course."

"Then can I see him?"

"When the time is right, I may bring him out to be yours. But my dear, I can tell you right now that when my kingdom is set up, he is one that will never submit to me. What am I to do with a servant who will not submit to my lordship? Do you not think it will be better for him to stay forever asleep than have his soul banished? Will you tolerate him staying in chains at your side?"

Unsurmountable guilt overwhelmed her. "Too many questions! I don't know what I've done. Did I do right or did I do wrong? I can't even think straight anymore," she whimpered in defeat.

Liel gave her a delicate smile in the mirror. She was lost and confused, exactly where he wanted her to be. This state made her vulnerable to him. Now it was time. "That is okay, my dear. There is no easy road to travel here. John made his choice. His decision to aid the enemy is not your burden to bear. It's mine. So release your guilt to me and rest in my peace. Surrender to me your worries and concerns and I promise you, that confusion will fade away."

Adriana closed her eyes and released all her guilt and her shame for having betrayed the one she claimed to love. Seductively, Liel took her soul and she willingly became one of his faithful servants, and she did this of her own accord. Brushing aside all the warnings from both her husband and her only daughter, Adriana chose another path, one she wanted to believe was the right path. When she opened her eyes, a strange sensation overcame her; it was filled with pride and confidence at what she had done. Without realizing what had happened to her, Adriana had become utterly bewitched by Liel's exceptionally well-played deception. She was now his.

As soon as she fully surrendered, all confusion left. Her love for her family turned into pity for their condemned souls. She no longer wrestled with the fact that one day she would need to aid in the capture of her own daughter. After all, it was clearly for Jen's benefit that she would be caught. If she would not choose Liel, then it would be her own undoing. Adriana came to understand that in the days to come, families would be split between sides. It was the way it was to be. Lucky for her, she thought, that she had at least chosen the right side. Liel circled to her side and extended his hand to her.

"Let's go now, my dear. I have had the news spread of your cunning work to manipulate John and lure him to us. I have called for a dinner celebration with all your fellow comrades that work alongside you. You are now their hero, one who has succeeded and they wish to admire you for your great accomplishments."

She smiled at him, the shame and guilt gone. If Liel was a creature of darkness, she reasoned, than why did she feel so good and accomplished at what she had done? Adriana boldly took hold of the hand that he had extended to her, "Yes, of course, Liel. I would be honored to see the others and dine with my comrades. Indeed; this is a great victory for us."

And with that, the two departed for their…dinner celebration.

Chapter 30
In the Days After

Days quickly turned into weeks, and weeks into months. Jen had become relentless, pursuing all aspects of her training. Before dawn she would rise and Iyon would pick her up and take to the sky. The combat training in the air was far from simple as they strategized on how to ambush Dunamis and Micol, who would be in hiding in order to ambush Iyon and Jen. The purpose of the constant regiment was to sharpen each other's skills in hopes of overcoming any future ambushes that could take them down. They fought each other with great intensity, both in ground and air combat. With blazing swords of blue fire and bolts of energy that came from the two Warriors, they attacked one another to the point where one team had no choice but to surrender. They learned to work as a team, backing each other up when they needed it. Just when Jen found herself under the blade of Micol, there was Iyon to defend her and ward off her opponent. All morning until afternoon, the two pairs advanced relentlessly, but in time, their hard work paid off as they soon became equals in the game of combat.

The day was split as Micol would go to the army camp and continue to oversee the combat training of his soldiers. Iyon would take Jen to the temple where she dove into the scrolls her father had studied. And then there were times she spent privately with Hope and the River Chest where she pushed herself far past human limitations to become what she needed to become.

. . . .

John's body shook with incredible violence while in his stasis. The red glow turned into a prickly hot oven that gave him great physical pain while Liel played with his mind. Liel wanted vengeance for losing Dangor and made John pay dearly for it.

Liel threatened John in every way imaginable, but John held fast. He was ready to die with his secret knowledge and Liel knew this.

Day by day I weaken you, John. I will find out everything I need to. The entrance to Tolare, where Hope is really hiding, and that cursed Chest. I want that chest. If you will not bring it to me, then Jen will. I have her now. She is in my possession. She screams your name, John. Should I tell her that her torment will not end because of your stubbornness?

John retaliated, *Everything that comes out of your mouth is a lie. You don't have Jen. You never will, nor will you have my secrets. You are a fool, Liel. When Dangor drew out my secrets, he took them all.*

You are a bad liar, John. Perhaps I will torture Adriana instead.

You will do what you must, but you will not have Tolare, or Hope, or the Chest. You might as well kill me. I will not bend to you.

You will break, if not to me, than you will to my queen.

Liel cut himself off from John's mind, letting the punishment of his prison chamber work on him for a while. Liel had little concern for the words that came out of John's mouth. John would submit; they all did in time. Meanwhile, Liel had many matters to attend to besides just one muck of a human.

Day in and day out, this was John's new life until the day he would finally surrender or die. There were no other options.

. . . .

The incredible strength of Dunamis united the army as never before. It was Iyon who noticed the growing union the army displayed with him. They were turning into an unstoppable force as they once were in the days of Soterios. Into the seventh week of their morning combat practice, Iyon made a clear decision. Before they parted ways, Iyon called out to his brother.

"Dunamis, before you go, there is something that must be decided."

Dunamis looked at his brother and knew what he was going to say. He could feel what Iyon was thinking, but let him speak his mind.

"Yes, brother, what is it that you feel must be decided?"

"There has never in history been two generals of the army. There simply cannot be. I am going to step down as General. I want you to take Father's place as I know Micol will take his father's place. I will make Hope aware of my decision and this will be announced to all of Tolare. The General and his army must be as one and I see that this great destiny truly lies with you and Micol."

"I see within you why you say that. You feel that your destiny lies with the Key Holder. I cannot agree nor disagree. I will submit to my destiny whatever it may be. We should let Hope have the final word."

"I see Soterios in you. All the land sees it and it brings us all a great strength. We will always work as one, but I see my place and accept it. Hope will have the final say, but we both know what that will be. I wanted this said between us before that decision was made."

Dunamis bowed his head and raised it back up. "A very honorable decision, Iyon."

Iyon nodded in respect and they parted ways with the ones they were destined to be with. From that day forward, though it was not officially announced, word among the city and the camp spread that Micol and Dunamis would be the next Captain and General of not only the army of Tolare, but one day would be in command of the united army of all the worlds of Earth. That day would not come unless the evil was purged once and for all from the land and only then would balance be restored.

After several months of intense training, Jen had fully transformed into a formidable and powerful weapon. What she accomplished in months should have taken years to achieve. This was something that Liel would not expect or see coming.

At the end of her sixth month of training Jen's eyes popped open in the wee early hours of the morning and felt a most incredible force calling out to her frantically.

Chapter 31
During the Days of Training

After Liel had imprisoned John, over the following months, he found himself enormously busy. He began to build his army in preparation for the takedown of Tolare. Then there was the daily torment of John, who proved to be a stronger human than he wanted to give him credit for. And there was the project he had with his secret workforce that needed daily attending to, in which he made the decision to promote Adriana to a place of leadership that she blindly and gratefully accepted. And lastly, there was the complicated and very calculated plan of the imminent destruction of the human race on True Earth, which to him was the ultimate prize that he unceasingly thirsted and hungered for. It wasn't the planet he wanted by any means; no, it was the souls of all the people. There was not a single human he wanted to escape from his clutches.

His patience was also running out because news of the abomination that was called Malum and the vortex had not been heard from for months now. As Liel hurried across the dark side of his underworld palace, he let his mind scan the worlds for Lawless. Was it hiding from him on purpose? The Master was growing weary of this. Then, he felt it.

No! It cannot be! There is no way any could have gotten to them! How is it I have not seen this until now?

Liel's clothes shredded off of him as he roared and transformed into his true dragon form. His body instantaneously grew to a great size; the biggest of all dragons. His scales were metallic black and glistened against the dark light of the night. The length of just one of his claws measured the length of a tall human male. The floor beneath him broke into pieces as he pounded through his castle halls.

Liel formed a portal of his own and sent himself to the Witch's Abyss, a dark realm he had created long ago where the witches could have a place of safety from the attacks of Hope, Iyon and the forces of good.

In moments, Liel arrived at the caverns that led to the home of the witches. He roared so loud that the entire realm shook and the tunnels almost broke apart as he called for them to come to him. They were like his children. He waited, he listened, but no one came. And then Liel put the pieces together. There was, after all, only one way any could have ever gotten to them.

Lawless! Lawless! Lawless!

Liel had enough. It was time to subdue it once and for all. It was now free and rightfully his for the taking as was told in the prophecy.

Liel embarked on a relentless pursuit of the vortex. Throughout the worlds of Earth Liel chased it from one world to the other and from one realm to the next. The pursuit lasted days as the great dragon hunted its prey. And then the day came when Liel was in the mountains of the Darth World that the dragon had finally caught up with it. The dragon enveloped it in fire and power to keep it from fleeing any longer.

"You will be mine! I will control you and you will do my bidding!"

The vortex wailed in terror as it wanted to be ruled by no one. It was free and wanted to stay that way. As a last resort, it called out to her.

. . . .

Jen! It is I, Lawless. Liel has cornered me. If he takes me I will become his slave and will have to do his bidding. Come to my aid now. If you do not, then things will only get worse for you. I am pinned up against the western mountains in the Darth world. Find me!

Remember this day, Lawless. You will owe me.

Within seconds, Jen had jumped out of bed, dressed and grabbed her weapons. She ran out the front door and delivered a disturbing message to Iyon.

I have to save Lawless from Liel by the western mountains of the Darth World. I will return!

Jen, no!

And she was gone.

. . . .

After all the months of training, Jen had no fear in facing the man-like creature that destroyed her family. She had worked through the bitterness and the rage and had learned to let that go. She had even learned the power of forgiveness to a being fully undeserving. It was not for his sake; no, not at all. It was for her freedom. She would deal with Liel today, but she would not allow him to speak his deceptive words to her. Her father had listened to him and had no choice but to surrender. Jen would not give Liel that room for talk. When she entered the Darth World, she saw the vortex pinned against the mountains as the dragon began to inhale. The vortex was about to get sucked into its fiery mouth.

She came up behind the great beast that towered over her and created a giant portal behind his back and then thrust it forward, completely engulfing the dragon. Liel never knew what hit him. In a second, he was transported into Shadow Earth, in the valley where the tree stump was incinerated by John. In seconds, he was back at the mountain and ready to fight, but there was no one to fight, and no vortex to declare as his. In his anger, he slashed at the mountains, cutting them to pieces.

Liel transported himself back to his own lair and morphed back into his human form so he would not do further damage to his palace. With a venomous will, he went to retrieve John. If John would not bow as his servant, then he would kill him by the day's end.

. . . .

Jen took the spinning vortex to the ruined city of Eshron. As soon as she arrived, she notified Iyon that she was safe from Liel.

"You are a strange abomination, Lawless," Jen said.

"I can see he is not in pursuit of me. He has turned his vengeance now toward another."

"He will take out his anger on my father. I cannot engage him face to face, I have been told not to do that yet. It's your turn to return the favor of your freedom today. Retrieve my father, and take him to Dagger's Edge before the Death Drop in Tranquil Earth. When I see him there I will take him from you. After that, my only suggestion to you is to run."

The spinning vortex that loomed in front of Jen said nothing in response; it just vanished, and so did Jen.

. . . .

The lever was pulled and the red glow that incased John in stasis lowered from the ceiling until it disappeared. Liel grabbed the chains and they disintegrated in his hands. John would have risen to the ceiling, but instead Liel grabbed John's leg and threw him across the room. John's body slammed against the wall and fell to the floor. His whole body hurt from the torturous pain he daily endured from the red glow. When he could finally open his eyes, the first thing he saw were eyes of fire, full of hatred and every form of malice.

"You underestimated her," John said proudly and with great boldness.

The man-like creature was so full of hate that he could not even speak to this human captive. Instead, he grabbed John and took him away through a portal. They ended up at the highest point of what was once a great city, Tran. John's hands were still cuffed and the leather strap tightly bound around his upper torso so that he could not move his arms.

Liel picked him up by the back of the strap and dangled him over the edge of the structure so he could see all the prisoners.

"If you do not reveal to me the doorway into Tolare and the secrets I demand to know, then every one of these captives below will taste the fire from my mouth. Every last one will see death and they scream your name as they burn"

. . . .

I'm back, Iyon. I am at the temple.

I sensed that you were and am almost there.

Jen looked to the sky and saw a flash of lightning heading her way. In a matter of seconds, Iyon landed at the center of the temple and glared heavily at Jen.

"That was a direct violation of the oath you gave to Hope. How could you risk punishment or correction at such a time as this?"

Jen approached the center and the two lowered into the dark abyss below. It immediately filled with light. The trunk of the tree split open, revealing the life source inside. Waves deep and heavy hit them both.

"Jen, what have you done?"

"I did not break my vow," Jen boldly said.

"You told Iyon you were going to save a creature from Liel that was undeserving of it. You gave your word that you would not face Liel until the right time. Today was not that day. The life force within the River Chest cannot be bound to one who does wrong."

Jen cut her off, "And I have done no wrong. You said not to face Liel and I did not. My attack came from behind. He never saw what was coming and I never saw his face. Therefore, the promise was kept."

"We must let the Ancient within the Chest judge. You have catapulted to a higher level with more responsibility and with that will come a greater measure of judgment on actions as well."

"I understand that, but according to the words of my oath, I did not break it. Let the River Chest see and judge."

The chest opened and soon Jen was encased inside its river of light. The Ancient spoke first to Jen. "An entire course of events have changed now, Jen. When Lawless reached out to you, what was it that made you decide on such a bold course of action?"

"You already know why, Ancient," Jen replied humbly, not disrespectfully, and solely with a purity of heart regarding the new relationship she had fashioned over the past months with the Ancient. Jen recently came to understand why the Chest asked these questions. It was because of the desire for that relationship to grow in strength, communication and trust. "I saw that if I saved Lawless then it would owe me, giving my father a chance to be saved without me having to break my oath. I know that though my training has prepared me well, the timing for that event must also fall into place. With a clear conscious I decided on the course of action. I have no regrets or guilt."

"Their union is unavoidable; still, the course of action shows no wrongdoing. You cleverly faced him without having to face him and have shown him that you have come far in your training. He will push harder now to attain what he so hungrily wants."

"Whether now or later what he strives for matters not. In one way or another, it was meant to be this way."

"Your way of thinking has worked. John is here on Tranquil Earth. Still, you cannot face Liel. Let us see what the anomaly called Lawless does now. If an opportunity arises to retrieve John, then take it. The decisions you made today are acceptable by the Ancient."

The river dissipated back into the Chest.

"The Ancient said his piece. Be wary of decisions like that in the future, Jen. We cannot risk losing you," was Hope's final word on the matter.

"I give my word. However, my actions have led Liel to bring John straight to us. I am confident Lawless will come through. One thing I have noticed about that strange anomaly; when it has a debt, it follows through. It is why I did what I did."

"If we leave Tolare," Iyon interrupted, "we can survey Tran. The gem has protected my presence from being detected throughout all of Tranquil Earth in the past."

"But Liel has never been here until now," Jen said. "He may sense what the others cannot."

"Or not," interjected Hope. "It has not been tried before. Perhaps it is time to try." From out of the portal floated another emerald-colored ring and fastened itself onto the ring finger of Jen's right hand.

"This will help protect you from detection. Go, and if he notices you, then leave immediately so that you do not engage him."

Just then, the platform began to lower, letting the outside light fill the cavern until another platform came from the side and took its place, enclosing everyone again. Iyon and Jen waited with great expectations of who they would see coming down.

"Going on a mission to Tran without us?" called Micol.

Jen beamed a smile, "Not a chance! And I see you two were eavesdropping."

"Dunamis has extremely good hearing."

Another ring for Micol floated from Hope's glow and then fashioned itself onto Micol's ring finger.

"Then it will be known after this day there are two of you. But remember, Liel cannot be engaged. Not under any circumstance."

"We understand," they all spoke at the same time.

With the plan set, Jen straddled Iyon, and Micol mounted Dunamis. Jen created a portal that led to the fields of Tranquil Earth and the team vanished from Hope's presence.

Soon? Hope asked.

Yes, very soon, replied the Ancient.

Chapter 32
And so it Came to Pass

The dragon had become obsessed with making John surrender his will to him now. He called for an assembly of the entire city to meet at the temple where all were forced to bend their knees to the Master that had subdued them. Dolorous came out of the black cloud and bowed to the Master and with him, all of the Skeign that were assigned to keep Tranquil Earth under control also bowed. A tall metal pole was erected at the top of the temple steps and a hook was placed at the top. The dragon hung John by the leather strap that was bound around his waist, for all to see.

Then the great and terrible Dragon stood behind the pole and towered far above it. He let out a thunderous roar that caused the city to shake and the slaves to quiver in fear.

Iyon and Dunamis were flying high in the sky and hiding in the violet clouds when Liel roared. The vibrations were felt through the air waves. They were flying directly over the city and peered straight down.

Emotions tried to overcome Jen when she saw her father on the pole.

"Hang on, Dad. We're coming."

"My slaves!" bellowed the dragon, "Because of the insolence of this one rebel and his refusal to submit and become my servant; today, you will all be executed."

The crowd could not speak as they were forcibly muted by Liel's obsessive need to control them, so all they could do was moan in misery.

"He's going to kill them all," said Dunamis.

"We have orders not to engage Liel," said Jen, "What are we going to do?"

"We're going to wait patiently and look to the north," Iyon said plainly.

"What?" That comment threw Jen off.

"Look to the north," Iyon said again.

They all turned. Massive dark clouds the size of mountains were forming. An enormous twister formed from the clouds, at least a mile in length. It was Lawless, and he was coming to make a stand against the dragon.

As Liel opened his jaws, about to incinerate the masses, a wind blew into the city, causing Liel to stop in his tracks. He turned and saw it.

"You have come to me. I see what you are doing, you rebellious servant." He whipped his massive head toward Dolorous and growled, "I will be right back." Liel spread his wings, each wingspan measuring hundreds of feet, and took to the sky. He was so preoccupied with Lawless and his need for control that he did not sense the Warriors' proximity.

The vortex stayed to the north in order to draw Liel far away from the city. The vortex spun so its deadly opening rose up to face the dragon head-on.

"We wait for them to collide," Micol ordered. "As soon as they do, Jen, you and Iyon go for John. Just transport him out of here and then I would like to leave a mark that Liel will never forget. Let us show him just what two Warriors and their fighters can do. Dunamis and I will attack Dolorous to give you time to rescue John."

"Let's do this. And if we can, let's take them all," Jen said.

"Is everyone ready?"

Eyes glowing, weapons drawn, and then the dragon and the vortex collided, creating the hideous sound of a sonic boom. What happened next took only minutes.

Dunamis and Iyon dropped out of the sky like lightning. By the time Dolorous looked up, Dunamis was already upon him and cut through half his body with a laser so sharp, his scales shredded from his body. It was a blow intended to kill him. Dunamis did not stop there. He slashed at him two more times, knocking out his feet and cutting him straight through the heart. Just before the attack on Dolorous, Micol jumped off of Dunamis and landed near the pole where he strategically attacked with his weapon, wiping out hundreds of Skeign per minute. Iyon flew to the top of the pole and sliced the leather straps holding John. As he fell, Iyon gently wrapped him in coils of blue energy that exuded from his eyes and carefully landed him on the ground. Jen did not waste a second. In an instant, the portal was created and Iyon carried him through. A second later, Iyon was back.

"The Captain was at the temple with a cot to transport John to Dahlia's," Iyon blurted out.

The Skeign covered the sky like a thick blanket and off in the distance, Liel roared fiercely as he now knew that the city was being ambushed while he was entangled with the raging vortex. In his great fury, Liel exhaled and blew a massive wave of heat and fire so strong that it broke the base of the twister in half, cutting the power of Lawless down as well. He heard the dying roar of Dolorous and took his anger out on the vortex. He opened his mouth and sucked the great vortex straight into it. Lawless was now helpless against the strength of the beast and was swallowed up. Soon Lawless and all of its ancient and unfathomable power began to unite with Liel, making him stronger than he ever was before.

Jen knew they had only seconds left and the team worked as one. Iyon and Dunamis flooded the sky with a giant wall of blue energy that covered over the people. All the Skeign that came into contact with it vaporized. Jen let the power of the Ancient flow through her and a portal was created long enough to scoop up all the captives that were in the assembly from one side all the way to the other. And then as she thrust her hands forward, the portal swooped across the assembly, transporting them all to Tolare.

The ground shook at the pounding of Liel's claws as they hit the earth. The team jumped through the portal. Jen shrank and closed the portal just as Liel flew like a monster over the city. He had claimed his prize, but it came to him at a great cost. Dolorous was lying dead on the temple floor where he had once proudly stood. Half of the army of Skeign creatures were gone and all of his slaves were taken, along with John. This is the devastation that two Warrior Horses, a Captain, and a Key Holder caused him.

In his great and horrible fury, Liel completely destroyed Tran that day. The entire city was demolished by flames and every building was smashed to the ground. Liel took the survivors of the Skeign army and departed from Tranquil Earth.

Chapter 33
The Fire in the Night

After many days of recovering, John got up in the night, walked into the field and dug a large fire pit. He gathered all the wood stocked outside the cabin that was meant for cooking and carried it out to the pit. His friends and comrades General Stantyon, Jared, Taq, and Fox had come to check on him and saw what he was doing. Without anyone saying a word, they all chipped in and began carrying wood to the pit. Jen emerged from the house and saw them working. She slipped on her moccasins and joined them. They worked for almost an hour until the wood was piled high. Dahlia walked up to the group in the field carrying a lit torch. She came to stand silent by John's side. After a few moments of silence, Iyon flew in with Zurina on his back and Dunamis carried Micol. His friends all came to stand by his side and then Dahlia handed the torch to John. He sullenly walked over to the pile of wood and lit it on fire.

The company of friends stood in silence and watched the fire consume the wood. It was an old ritual John learned from Tolarian history that was done when loved ones had died, but not in a natural way. John covered his face with his hands and Jen wrapped her arms around him.

It was a truth that had been finally accepted. Adriana had pledged her soul to Liel. She was gone for good, and there could be no rescue. It was an eternal decision that she had willingly made.

The fire of the night filled the Tolarian sky. As the wood crackled and the sparks flew into the air, it carried on its crimson lights the burial of Adriana Hanning, wife to John and mother to Jen. And that is how the night ended, in a pure and utterly bittersweet truth that not everyone takes the right path.

....

In the immediate days after Liel's humiliating defeat, Liel had locked himself in one of his throne rooms deep within the castle of the underworld. He had finally obtained the anomaly named Lawless that he had patiently waited on for centuries and should have been celebrating, but instead, he sat on his throne with a blank stare of complete shock upon his face at what the four had taken from him. Dolorous was an ancient dragon, undefeated in every battle he had ever fought. Liel scoffed at his own foolishness for taking John out of stasis. What a trophy he had lost! And what a fool they made him out to be in front of his own subjects.

The sound of high powered heels came from the hall. Liel ordered that none disturb him or he would devour them, and yet, this foolish woman boldly walked into his presence. He grimaced in delight as it reminded him of how bold Dolorous had always been. The woman in the black gown approached his throne. It was Adriana. She had a smile of foolish confidence as she approached her Master. She walked straight up the steps to the throne and bent down to stare directly into Liel's face.

"Time to stop pouting, my king. I found a little something for you," she said with a smile.

The side chamber door opened and there, standing in the entrance, was Dangor.

Liel stood to his feet and walked straight to the beast. Dangor bowed his head to the ground.

"My servant, I've assigned subjects to search all the realms and worlds of Earth for you. You can tell me that story later. What I want to know is...do you have his secrets?"

"Yes, Master. I have all of his secrets."

With eyes of fire accompanied with a wicked smile and a vengeance that filled his blackened soul, Liel gave the command.

"Then it's time to gather all my army. Tolare…will be mine."

www.ingramcontent.com/pod-product-compliance
Lightning Source LLC
Chambersburg PA
CBHW061136200626
46817CB00016B/1671